JENNIFER S. ALDERSON

The Vermeer Deception

First published by Traveling Life Press 2020

Second edition

ISBN: 9789083001166

This book was professionally typeset on Reedsy.
Find out more at reedsy.com

Contents

1

The First Signs of Spring

Kurt Weber gazed out the tenth-story window, taking in the first leaves of spring budding on the tree outside his doctor's office. The lilting melody of a robin flying away from its nest on a lower branch made him turn. Snuggled up inside were three perfect eggs—the ultimate symbol of new life. How ironic.

"Herr Weber, did you hear me? I am afraid there is nothing more we can do. Your cancer has spread too rapidly." The doctor was young, too young to understand what Kurt was feeling inside.

Kurt nodded, keeping his gaze directed outside at the bright sun and clear blue skies. He had never noticed the beauty of nature before—such a shame.

"I have informational pamphlets for you to take home. Our grief counselors and pain managers will want to make appointments with you in the coming weeks. We want to do everything we can to help you—"

"You've done all that you could, and I appreciate it." Kurt's voice cracked as he spoke. He had been battling lung and prostate cancer for several years now. He knew this day would come, but that knowledge did not make his imminent death any easier to process.

"Do you have a lawyer to help get your affairs in order?"

"I do." *Several, in fact,* Kurt thought. Most of what he had to get in order before he passed, however, he couldn't share with his regular legal team. "How much time do I have?"

The robin's sweet melody attracted their attention to the tree, and together, they watched as the mother bird returned to her nest and gently settled her tiny body over her eggs.

"We never know for certain, but I estimate three months. If you are lucky."

Kurt's shoulders hunched over. The doctor's words were a punch in the gut. Three months wasn't long. He knew he should have already prepared for this day, but it was too difficult to face the inevitable. Yet his impending demise required that he act—and quickly. He couldn't leave his father's artwork behind for the Network to take.

He chewed on his lip as the unanswered question that had haunted him for months resounded again in his head. To whom could he entrust the three hundred and fifty-seven looted masterpieces that his father had saved from the Nazis during World War II?

2

The Lost Vermeer

"Hey, Vincent. Good to hear from you. Are you back in Amsterdam?" Zelda Richardson asked. She had not spoken to her boss, Vincent de Graaf—a private investigator specializing in art recovery—in three weeks. Since opening a second office in Split, Croatia five months ago, he preferred email and text messages to phone conversations.

"I got back last week, but Theresa and I needed a bit of us-time."

Vincent was such a workaholic, Zelda was surprised he had taken any time off. Then again, she never figured she would hear him utter the phrase "us-time." Even though he had been planning to open a second office for more than a year, she could imagine settling into a new routine was tough on both him and his wife, Theresa.

"But I'm back at work now," her boss continued. "Based on your progress reports, it sounds like you've made quite a bit of headway since we last spoke. Is there anything you want me to take a look at while I'm here? What are you working on right now?"

"I'm writing up a summary of my provenance research into the Henri Matisse oil. I think I've found enough for you to prove it's the real deal." Vincent's bread and butter were cases such as the one she was currently working on. Before handing over millions of euros for a painting, wealthy clients would hire Vincent to check the work's provenance to ensure they were not buying a fake or something stolen.

"Excellent. My client will be thrilled."

"I should be able to finish the report tomorrow. The Matisse is the last of the seven cases you assigned to me."

"That's great news. That means I'll be able to bill them this month. I could use the cash."

"Still no joy in Croatia?" Zelda knew Vincent had been approached to investigate several local thefts since his office in Split opened, yet he had not been able to find a viable lead in any of the cases. Though he hadn't explicitly said so, Vincent's expectation that he would be able to solve cases more quickly if located in Eastern Europe didn't seem to have been met. At least, not yet. She hoped Vincent would soon catch a break. One success would give his new office the marketing boost it needed and him the confidence to keep at it.

"Nope, no joy. Say, it sounds like you have time for lunch. Why don't you come up to the house? Theresa is cooking paella."

Alarm bells went off in Zelda's mind. Who cooked such a complicated dish for lunch? Someone who wanted to have a romantic meal with their partner, she figured.

"Are you sure? Maybe you should enjoy lunch with your wife, instead. I can swing by after you are done."

"There's no time. I'll explain when you get here, but this might be our last chance to chat face-to-face for a while. Theresa understands."

Zelda wondered whether she did. Since Vincent opened his second office, his relationship with his wife had been a bit rocky. Zelda understood Theresa's frustration; during the past few months, her husband had spent far more time in Eastern Europe than in Amsterdam.

"When can you come over? I still have to pack," Vincent said. Based on his irritated tone, Zelda figured he was checking his watch as he spoke.

"If you are certain she won't mind, then I'll be right over."

"Great, see you in a few minutes."

Two hours later, Zelda finished her second serving, thoroughly sated. It was the best paella she had ever eaten. Unfortunately she wasn't able to compliment the cook. By the time she had arrived at Vincent's home, Theresa had already left to go shopping.

Between scrumptious bites of rice and seafood, she and Vincent had spent the afternoon updating each other about their progress in their current projects. Despite the many difficulties he was experiencing getting his new office up and running, it sounded like Vincent's luck was starting to change for the better. Last night, a Croatian contact let him know that one of the suspects Vincent was looking for was back in Split.

"So I'll be flying back to Croatia tonight instead of Friday," he said, rounding off his update.

"Hence, the paella and shopping," Zelda muttered. Theresa must have made the extravagant lunch to celebrate their last afternoon together—and then gone shopping because she was furious with Vincent for spending that time with Zelda instead.

"What?" Vincent asked, a quizzical expression on his face.

"Oh, sorry. It's nothing." She blushed, hoping he could not read her mind. His relationship with his wife was his business, not hers. "Tell you what, why don't we finish up so you can spend some time with Theresa before you leave."

"There's no time for that, but I should start packing. Is there anything else we need to hash out in person? I'll be checking email regularly but would rather save telephone conversations for emergencies. I usually have the ringer off, anyway."

She smiled, knowing that Vincent hated telephones on a good day. "No problem. Since I'm about to finish all of my current projects, I was wondering what my next assignment might be. The phones aren't exactly ringing off the hooks."

"Once you finish up the reports, it might be quiet for a few days. Though you never know when the next client will get in touch."

Zelda sucked up her courage before daring to again ask about the mystery project he had mentioned several months ago. So far, every time she broached the subject, he shut the conversation down.

"Well then, maybe I can start looking for your friend's Vermeer?"

Soon after they returned from Turkey, Vincent had told Zelda about a portrait by Johannes Vermeer that an old friend of his was searching for, but before they could discuss the specifics, he had flown out to Split, chasing after a new job. Before leaving, he had instructed her to start on the backlog of provenance research he had left behind and told her that he would send her the information about the Vermeer, as soon as he had received all of it from his friend. Days later, he had instead sent a cryptic message making clear that his friend's Vermeer would have to wait. Since then, he bristled anytime she mentioned it.

"Oh, yeah, Huub just asked for a progress report last week. I did promise him that we would check that lead, and I guess this is as good a time as any for you to do so," Vincent said, referring to Huub Konijn, Zelda's old boss and a curator at the Jewish Historical Museum. He drummed his fingers on the table as he stared out the window, seemingly lost in thought.

Zelda eyed her boss critically. "I have to say, this is not like you. Normally you would be chomping at the bit if you thought you were on the trail of a painting as unique as a Vermeer. But you are acting like searching for it is an inconvenience. What gives?"

Her boss let out a long sigh and shrugged. "You got me there. I have to level with you—I don't think we should search for this painting, but Huub promised Roelf that we would, and I feel obligated to help."

"But you were so eager to find it a few months ago. What changed your mind?"

"In his enthusiasm to get us to check this lead, Roelf led Huub and me to believe that his proof of ownership was more conclusive. After I saw the dossier, I changed my mind, but Huub had already assured Roelf we would follow up on it. However, since Huub is still in London working on that new exhibition, he hasn't had the chance to visit The Hague's archives, either."

"So if you think checking this lead is a simple as visiting an archive, why didn't you ask me to do so a few months ago—if anything else, just to get it over with?"

Vincent leaned over the kitchen table and locked eyes with her. "Because

I am convinced that finding the Vermeer will only lead to more heartache. Roelf's proof is so flimsy that I don't think it will stand up in court. Which means that even if we somehow find the painting, it would take another miracle for him to actually get it back. Roelf is already so ill, finding the Vermeer and then having his claim rejected would most likely kill him."

Zelda's eyebrows crinkled as she took in her boss's conundrum.

"However, I don't like to renege on my word," her boss continued, apparently unaware of Zelda's growing discomfort. "Which is where you come in."

"So who is your friend exactly?"

"His name is Roelf Konig, and he was born in Berlin in 1931 to a Dutch Protestant father and German Jewish mother. He and his older sister were sent to live with his aunt in Los Angeles in 1938 when anti-Semitism had intensified in Germany. His parents didn't join them because his father owned sugar factories in Germany, Belgium, and the Netherlands and didn't want to leave Europe."

"That had to be tough on both the kids and parents. Did his parents make it through the war?"

Vincent shook his head. "After Roelf and his sister left for the States, his parents fled to Amsterdam, figuring they would be safer there. They were, until the occupying Nazi force found Jewish families hiding in one of their Dutch factories in 1942. His parents were arrested, and their businesses and personal possessions were confiscated. That's when the Vermeer disappeared. Roelf's dad was deported to a work camp, and his mother to Ravensbrück, a concentration camp for women. Neither of his parents survived."

"That's horrible. Roelf didn't even get a chance to know his parents." Zelda pushed her disgust aside as her resolve to find his missing painting intensified. She couldn't change the past, but she might be able to help reunite Roelf with a piece of his family's history. "Tell me about their art collection."

"His mother came from old money and had inherited an extensive art collection—some three hundred paintings created by renowned artists. When they left Germany, they took their favorite five paintings with them and arranged for the rest to be shipped over a week later. The crates were packed and booked for transport but never arrived. As soon as the Nazi government found out his parents had left the country, they leveraged a property tax on their home. Since his parents were gone, the Nazis chose to confiscate their house and everything inside in lieu of payment. A week later, anything of value was sold at auction."

Zelda couldn't believe what she was hearing. "A property tax? Why would they do that?"

"Because Roelf's mother was Jewish and fleeing the country. The Nazi party invented special taxes such as that one to justify their seizure of their victims' possessions. It was a fate that overcame countless German Jews when they left their fatherland."

As always when she was discussing WWII looting cases with Vincent, she could feel her blood beginning to boil.

"The five paintings Roelf's family had brought to Amsterdam were far too valuable to be destroyed, yet no artwork was listed on the inventory list created by the Puls Moving Company when their home was cleared," Vincent continued. "Which leads me to believe the art was taken by an agent of the Mühlmann Agency."

"That was a clearinghouse for looted artwork—right?" Zelda asked.

"That is correct. It was named after its leader, Kajetan Mühlmann. The group of art historians and gallery owners who worked as their agents were tasked with sorting through any artwork that had been confiscated from Nazi victims. The best pieces were set aside for the Führermuseum, and the rest were sold off at auction and the money funneled back into the Nazi party. Most of the paintings stolen in the Netherlands and Belgium were brought to collection points created by the Mühlmann Agency before being dispersed."

"Do you mean to tell me that the Nazi party had been profiting off of the same artwork they claimed to despise? And here I thought that radical organizations such as ISIS were the first to steal and sell artistic treasures to fund their terrorism."

Vincent's laugh was low and bitter. "If only that were so."

"So what is the new lead?"

"The American private detective Roelf hired to search for the missing five paintings managed to locate four of them in different private collections. Unfortunately, Roelf lost all four restitution cases because the courts ruled that the owners had bought the paintings in 'good faith,' meaning neither the seller nor buyer could have known the paintings were stolen at the time of purchase."

Zelda's eyebrows shot up. "How could they not know the paintings were looted?"

"In all four cases, the current owners had documentation proving they had purchased the artwork from respected American art dealers many years earlier. Most looted art changed hands so often that the path back to the rightful owner it was stolen from is nearly impossible to trace. However, in this case, Roelf's detective was able to trace the paintings' histories back to their entry into the United States. A New York City gallery purchased all four from the Van Marle & Bignell auction house in The Hague in June 1942."

Zelda snapped her fingers. "I know I've heard you mention that name before."

"Van Marle & Bignell were known for working with the Nazi party, and many of the works confiscated by the Mühlmann Agency were auctioned off to foreign buyers there."

"What exactly am I looking for? I mean, you know as well as I do that Vermeer was an artist Hitler admired, so Roelf's portrait would have been earmarked for the Führermuseum, right?"

"Possibly, yet the Monuments Men didn't find it, nor has any documentation turned up that could explain what happened to it. Roelf is convinced that the person who brought his other four paintings to auction may be one of the few who know what happened to the Vermeer. And he may be right—if one of Mühlmann's agents confiscated all five paintings."

Zelda nodded slowly, turning over the information and reasoning in her mind. As weak as this lead was, it did sound like it was worth pursuing. "What do you think?"

"That it is a long shot," Vincent admitted. "It is entirely possible that one art dealer did take all five from Roelf's family home and made a notation in his business documentation about what he had done with the Vermeer. But even if we find that name—which is what you will be searching for in The Hague—then there is no guarantee that the person is still alive, that their archives survived the war unscathed, or that their relatives will know what had happened to Roelf's artwork."

"There are a lot of ifs in this equation," Zelda muttered.

"True, just as in every investigation I take on. However, if you can find out who brought the four paintings to auction, we may be one step closer to locating the Vermeer. Once you have visited the archive, let's talk again and discuss our next move."

Zelda felt a familiar rush of adrenaline as her mind started turning over the possibilities. "It sounds fascinating. I'll get started straight away," she said, then frowned as a realization entered her brain. "Oh, wait. My parents are arriving this weekend so I probably won't be able to make much headway until after they leave."

"Whoa, not so fast. I did promise Huub we would follow up on this lead, but finishing up your other assignment is your priority."

"I'll get that last report to you by Friday."

"Excellent. Thanks."

"So what can you tell me about this missing Vermeer?"

"It was one of his tronies, a portrait he'd made as a marketing ploy to show off his talents to potential customers. *Girl with a Pearl Earring* was also a tronie."

"Seriously? I would never have guessed. It's such a beautiful portrait."

"True, but it was painted as an advertisement of his skills. The tronie Roelf's mother inherited is one of a young woman wearing a ruby pendant. I'll email you the dossier before I fly out. The National Art Archives in The Hague may contain the information you need. It has a plethora of documents about the art dealers, experts, curators, and auction houses active in the 1940s."

Vincent glanced at his watch. "Theresa should be home any minute. Do you mind taking off? I need to finish packing so she can drive me to Schiphol before traffic gets too crazy."

"No problem. Hey, thanks for trusting me with this assignment."

"Thank you for tackling this, but don't beat yourself up if you run into a brick wall. I don't expect you to find anything."

"Thanks for that vote of confidence."

"Because I doubt all of their auction catalogs from the 1940s have been saved," Vincent said with a laugh. "I am certain that if there's anything there, you will find it. Have fun with your parents. We'll talk again after they've flown back to the States."

Zelda grinned from ear to ear. "Thanks, Vincent."

3

Upholding Family Honor

"I want out. I don't want to be a part of this crazy circle of old Nazis."

"Network, not circle, Gunther," Max Wolf—the self-appointed leader of the group—said.

Kurt Weber sat quietly, wondering whether Gunther knew what he was up against. If only his father had prepared him better, perhaps he wouldn't act so rashly.

Instead of injecting himself into the conversation, Kurt chose to stand and warm his hands by the hearth. The logs in the fireplace crackled and sparked as they burned, a touch too wet but necessary to heat the small cabin. Nights in the Bavarian Alps were still cold despite the arrival of spring. He expected there to be ice on his windshield when they departed.

"And we aren't crazy Nazis, nor were our grandparents," Max continued. "They were protectors of the arts and culture, people who dared to take action to safeguard what they loved and admired. The paintings and sculptures were otherwise destined to be destroyed by Hitler's regime. We cannot dishonor our forefathers' names by allowing the liberal media to brand them as fascists, thieves, traitors, or profiteers."

"I don't care what you call yourselves. I don't want to have any part in this. What was my father thinking? I thought his moral compass was sounder than this."

Whether Gunther shook his head in disgust or disappointment, Kurt couldn't tell. Not that it mattered. Either way, it was clear the Network had a serious problem on its hands.

Kurt's father had been a good friend of Gunther's dad, who often complained about his son's rebellious behavior and expressed worry as to how Gunther would react when he discovered the truth about their vast art collection. When his father tried to explain how it had come into their family's possession, Gunther only heard the word "Nazi" and tuned out the rest. Days later, he moved to Paris to study art history and, soon after, broke all contact with his family.

Years later, Gunther's father learned through mutual acquaintances that his son had married a Jewish woman and they were raising their children in her faith. It was no wonder his father never found the right moment to again try to explain his art collection's checkered past to his son.

Kurt watched as Max glared across the table at Gunther. Although Max was easily twenty years younger than his target, his gaze reminded Kurt of a father about to scold a naughty child. "There was nothing wrong with your father's morals. On the contrary, he did his utmost to protect your family's reputation by keeping the artwork that your grandfather saved safely stored away."

"You mean concealing it from their rightful owners so he could profit from the sales," Gunther spat at Max, clearly not intimidated. "My father was too cowardly to tell me everything in person, but he did leave a letter detailing how the artwork came into my grandfather's possession, as well as how this Network of yours works. I know how you sell the paintings to other complicit dealers and collectors. What disturbs me most is the sheer number of those willing to buy works they know are looted. It's shameful."

As Max's brow furrowed, Kurt realized he was about to shift tactics. The man was a chameleon. Before he could respond, the woman to his left placed a hand on his knee and squeezed. Brigitte sat regally on the edge of her stool, her petite frame barely filling it. They locked eyes and exchanged smiles. Kurt always suspected that they were a couple. Lord knows they were perfectly suited for each other. Both were goal-oriented sociopaths who valued money above all else.

"Your father did his utmost to keep the existence of our Network secret. Because he knew we have to be able to rely on each other for discretion and support." Max's eyes rested on Brigitte as he spoke. He placed a hand on hers. "There aren't many of us left."

Kurt glanced around at the thirteen men and women seated around the long table, all blood relatives of the original Network of art dealers who intentionally hid looted artwork from the Third Reich to prevent it from either being destroyed or sold abroad. At sixty-nine years old, Kurt was the oldest member and the last of the second generation. The others, all aged between twenty-seven and fifty-five, were the third generation. Most had not even met the grandparent they were still loyal to.

Though their forefathers' initial action could be applauded, their good deeds were tempered by the fact that none relinquished the artwork to the Allies after the Second World War ended. Instead, they kept these collections of masterpieces hidden away, leaving their relatives in a quandary. It was impossible to return the artwork without tarnishing their families' names because it had been too long ago to justify their relatives' decisions to hang onto it. And they were unable to show it to the public or sell it via reputable auction houses for the same reasons.

The only real option was to keep it hidden away or sell it off to those willing to keep their purchases hidden away from the public eye. When members of the Network died off without leaving heirs, their artwork was "adopted" by the others "to keep it in the family," as Max's father had liked to say. Over the years, the original Network of fifty-two had been reduced to fourteen, and each remaining member's collection had grown exponentially.

When those who did have offspring passed away, their heirs were invited to take their places within the Network. Up until now, all of the invitees had done so willingly, eager to connect with wealthy and discreet buyers. Gunther was proving to be the exception.

"I didn't ask to be a part of this," he protested.

"No, you didn't," Max soothed. "You can always hand over your father's collection to us and step away."

"No! It will disappear into your secret storage units." Gunther looked around the table, making eye contact with the others. "Did you know my wife hired a lawyer last year to find her family's collection of looted art?"

Murmurs of surprise went around the table, but Kurt knew it was all for show. Gunther's father had informed the Network last year, and had even provided them all with a list of the artwork she was searching for, but he'd never asked for its return. Kurt assumed the announcement was a warning to those who had any of her pieces to sell them abroad as quickly as possible.

"If you can provide me with a list of the art your wife is searching for, we can all check our records and see if we know more about the paintings' current whereabouts."

"That's not good enough! It's not just my wife—it's all the families we've wronged," Gunther roared, pounding a fist onto the table. "Ever since Dad died and his lawyer delivered this letter explaining his role in this historical tragedy, I have nightmares that the detective my wife hired will come knocking on our door."

He tore at his hair, his face a mask of helplessness. "It preys on my mind—all those victims of Nazi looting. So many families are hiring private detectives to search for the artwork you are hiding. And for what? So you can sell a piece whenever you want to buy a new car or a second home? Our forefathers saved it from being destroyed by the Nazis, which is admirable, but when they chose not to return it, they became profiteers. Which is what we all are. New restitution cases appear every week. There is still time to do the right thing and return the artwork to its rightful owners."

Kurt Weber listened intently to the young man's passionate speech. Even since coming face-to-face with his mortality, he had been contemplating similar actions. His father had risked so much to save hundreds of paintings—but to what end?

"What if I donate my grandfather's collection to a regional museum and provide them with the documentation he saved?" Gunther pressed when no answer was forthcoming. "The authorities would have no reason to investigate further. You would all be safe, and I could sleep again at night."

"That is not an option," Brigitte stated. "It is unfortunate that your father didn't explain more about the Network to you. We did try to return several small collections of artwork in the past, but all it did was revive worldwide interest in looted art. We cannot risk one of us being exposed."

Gunther shook his head in disgust as he pushed his chair away from the table. When he stood up, his whole body was trembling. "I need time to take this all in before I decide what to do."

Max nodded. "Of course. It is a crucial decision. But do also consider how your actions would affect the rest of us. It's not your art to dispose of as you see fit."

Gunther glared at him. "You're just as bad as Dad! You will never agree to return any of the artwork, will you?" When Gunther looked to the others, no one made eye contact with him. Even Kurt dared not look up, in case Max and Brigitte were keeping tabs.

"Of course not. It's your livelihood," Gunther continued, despair in his voice. "God forbid you might have to earn your keep. Holding onto the art is a choice, not a requirement. Our forefathers saved this art from certain destruction, so in that sense, they are heroes. There must be a way to explain their actions, both during and after the war. It's not too late to return the artwork. It will never be too late."

His impassioned plea moved Kurt, but as he looked around the table and saw the masks of indifference, he realized he was the only one.

Gunther must have noticed, as well. "I'm wasting my breath." When he stormed out of the room, Max was on his heels. Kurt resisted the temptation to follow them, knowing it would only bring trouble if he did.

Max trailed Gunther to the front door.

Two of his beefiest bodyguards were standing in front of it, blocking Gunther's exit. Max always brought them along to ensure their meetings would not be disturbed. He also hoped their presence would impress upon the rest of the Network how important it was to keep their secret safe.

"Call off your goons," Gunther growled.

"Let him pass, gentlemen," Max said.

The open cabin door brought in a whoosh of cold wind and smattering of snow. Max watched as Gunther jumped into his Maserati and sped away without a backward glance.

Max turned to the two men, both loyal employees. "Please make sure Gunther does not arrive home."

They nodded in acknowledgment.

Max turned on his heel and returned to the others.

4

A Nazi Art Clearinghouse

Zelda sipped her coffee while skimming the sheets of paper she'd just printed off, wondering what she was missing. *Maybe there is another attachment to Vincent's email,* she thought, but a quick search of her inbox was in vain. These eight printouts were all she had to go on.

Because she had finished her assignments for Vincent earlier than expected, Zelda had decided to read up on the Vermeer case before deep-cleaning her apartment. She knew she should have waited to open the dossier until after her parents' visit, but her curiosity had been in overdrive since her conversation with her boss.

Though he had repeatedly stated that Roelf's proof was flimsy, Zelda had assumed that Vincent was being his usual pessimistic self. Yet reading through the dossier had not eased her mind. After she had looked over the meager documentation and the photos provided, Zelda wondered whether she should even bother searching for the Vermeer. No court of law would return the painting to Roelf, not based on the three family photos he had provided as evidence of his mother's ownership.

Zelda glanced again at the snapshots taken in their family's living room, where the Vermeer was clearly visible in the background, hanging on the wall behind their couch. Also attached to the email was a single photograph of the Vermeer in its entirety. Zelda picked up the close-up, taking in the young woman's surprised expression. It was quite similar in composition to *Girl with a Pearl Earring*, though this one featured a dark-haired beauty wearing peasant's clothing and a large pendant around her neck.

Intrigued by what Vincent had told her about tronies, Zelda had searched online and found out quite a bit about the once-popular marketing technique. Vermeer painted several of these tronie portraits, mostly of women dressed in theatrical costumes and jewelry. He chose patterns and designs that showcased his incredible talent with light and reflection.

In Roelf's Vermeer, the model gazed at the viewer in astonishment, as if the painter had snuck up on her while she was dressing. The young woman was wearing a peasant's dress, and hanging around her neck was a large ruby pendant. Her curly hair was held back with a tortoiseshell comb. Even in black and white, the comb and necklace were so realistic, Zelda felt as if she could pull them out of the painting and wear them.

After she studied the photograph, Zelda reread the information Roelf's private detective had discovered, which had set this whole process in motion. In a New York gallery's historical archives, he had found the original receipt for the purchase of the four paintings taken from Roelf's family home. The name and address of the Van Marle & Bignell auction house in The Hague and the date of the sale were listed. That would be her starting point.

If the Dutch National Archives contained any of Van Marle & Bignell's wartime catalogs or business ledgers, there was a chance she would discover who brought the paintings to auction. Zelda now grasped why Roelf wanted this lead checked out yet also understood Vincent's hesitation. He said the information about Dutch dealers and auction houses held at the national archives was limited to whatever documentation was saved after the war ended. Until Zelda dove into its collection, they would have no way of knowing whether the paperwork they sought was stored in The Hague.

At first, Zelda had been surprised to learn that the paintings had been sold abroad. Because of the mass burnings of works created by Jewish authors and artists at the beginning of the war, she had always thought the Nazis burned or destroyed any degenerate artwork they confiscated. Yet that appeared not to be entirely accurate.

In 1938, Joseph Goebbels organized the first of many degenerate art auctions, offering up masterpieces by Marc Chagall and the like on the international market for next to nothing. He discovered that these "perversions to society" were the same paintings and sculptures non-German collectors swooned over and willingly paid hard cash for. They were snapped up immediately, no questions asked. And foreign currency was so much stronger than reichsmarks. In 1942, Hermann Göring issued a formal decree stating that all artwork deemed suitable for Adolf Hitler's planned Führermuseum should be earmarked for it. The rest should be either traded for the kind of artwork favored by the Nazis or sold abroad, with the profits funneled back into the Third Reich's coffers. That was where the Mühlmann Agency came in.

Too many paintings had been sold for a fraction of their worth, many destined for American art galleries where they were sold on to important art collectors and even museums—all unaware of the paintings' dark histories. It was so depressing.

Mühlmann's name also brought up a link to the Vlug Report, a detailed report about the activities of the *Dienststelle Mühlmann* that was completed in December 1945 by Captain Jean Vlug, a Dutch intelligence officer and captain in the Royal Netherlands Army, for the fine arts section of the Dutch Restitutions Committee. It also included inventories of art objects purchased, stolen, or confiscated in areas under German occupation.

The report gave her a clear description of the man behind the Nazi organization's art looting program: "Rotterdam was still burning when Kajetan Mühlmann, in his SS uniform, arrived in Holland to take up his new task as Chief of the Dienststelle... He is obstinate, has no conscience, and does not care about Art."

Those interviewing Mühlmann called him "a liar and a vile person," characterizing him as one of the greatest art thieves among the Nazis—and possibly ever. His agency's plundering in the Netherlands and throughout occupied Europe was prolific and wide-reaching.

During these postwar interviews, Mühlmann explained how many of the objects confiscated by his agency were then sold at auction houses located in the Netherlands, Germany, and Austria. In the report, other German officers expressed regret that so many works were sold to buyers in the United States, England, and France.

The Vlug Report also included a long list of Dutch dealers, agents, galleries, and auction houses that worked for and with the Mühlmann Agency. During the war, a select group of art dealers was allowed to take pieces out of the agency's confiscated collection and sell them, preferably abroad. Zelda was disgusted to learn these compliant dealers received twenty-five percent of the profits while the rest was funneled back to the Third Reich.

Zelda skimmed through the long list of names until she found Van Marle & Bignell, the auction house Roelf's parents' artwork passed through. According to the Vlug Report, it was one of two auction houses frequently used by agents of the Mühlmann Agency to liquidate artwork confiscated or stolen from Dutch citizens during the war.

Now that she knew what kind of auction house this was, it gave a clearer picture of what to expect whenever she had a chance to visit The Hague.

Zelda leaned back, turning all of this information around in her head. She only hoped she could find out who brought the paintings to the auction house so long ago. Whoever it was, they may be the only person who knew what had happened to Roelf's Vermeer after it was confiscated.

5

Degenerate Art

Zelda rubbed her eyes and choked back a cough. She didn't want to irritate the other researchers studying in the reading room of the National Archives in The Hague, but she couldn't help herself. The purified air always wreaked havoc on her sinuses.

Motivated by her interest in learning more about the Vermeer, Zelda had cleaned her apartment in record time, leaving a free day for a trip to The Hague. Even though she knew her boss wasn't expecting her to do anything until after her parents left, Zelda didn't want to wait two weeks to see whether the archives held any information useful in their search for the Vermeer.

Finding out who had brought Roelf's four paintings to auction had been surprisingly easy, though time-consuming. A helpful archivist found eleven boxes full of documents relating to the auction house, including 270 of its catalogs. However, none had been digitalized or indexed, meaning Zelda spent a long day slowly sifting through the delicate volumes in search of the correct date and sale. After lunch and two coffee breaks, she had found what she had been looking for. When she found Roelf's paintings mentioned in the catalog for the auction held in June 1942, she whooped in delight, garnering evil stares from her fellow researchers.

According to the catalog, the four paintings were brought in by Neue Gallery, Amsterdam. Armed with a name and date, the archivist soon discovered who ran the gallery at the time. Zelda couldn't believe their good fortune.

"It was owned by Bruno Weber, a German national. Both the gallery and its owner are on the ALIU Red Flag Names List. So is Van Marle & Bignell."

"What is that?"

"It's a list compiled by the Allies' Art Looting Intelligence Unit between 1944 and 1946. Any persons or businesses suspected of having worked with the Nazis were flagged for investigation. Let me get the auction house file for you. I'll also see what I can find out about Bruno Weber and his gallery."

"Excellent, thank you."

While waiting for the archivist to check her files, Zelda popped onto the internet and quickly discovered that Neue Gallery had locations in Amsterdam, Munich, and Berlin during the 1940s. Until 1977, it was owned solely by Bruno Weber. For now, Zelda would have to assume he brought Roelf Konig's paintings to auction.

Figuring the archivist would be back any minute, Zelda skimmed the many links her search query had found. There were articles about Bruno Weber being convicted of selling forgeries and the closure of his Munich gallery in 1977. Zelda added it to her list of things to investigate. There were current links to a Neue Gallery in Munich, but the website was quite sparse.

Before Zelda could read more, the archivist returned with several files. "Here you go. This is all I could find."

"Thank you," Zelda murmured as she took in the thin files. By the look of it, she wouldn't have to spend much more time in The Hague.

Zelda opened the file on Van Marle & Bignell first. According to the documents inside, thousands of confiscated paintings and sculptures were sold abroad via the auction house. Apparently, there were many foreign gallery owners and art dealers willing to ignore the dark history of these paintings.

Much of the degenerate art sold abroad ended up in a handful of New York-based galleries, which then sold it on to collectors and cultural institutions all over the United States, effectively whitewashing the artwork of its Nazi past.

That explains how Roelf's family's artwork ended up in New York, she thought.

As Zelda read further through the auction house file, she learned that Weber was one of several gallery owners who made their living reselling looted paintings through Van Marle & Bignell.

Next up was Bruno Weber. She quickly read through the thin file, containing primarily a few pages of biographical information. There wasn't much to learn about the art dealer. He was born in Berlin in 1898 and married a local woman in 1920. Shortly after, he opened his first gallery in what would later become East Berlin. In 1938, he opened a second gallery in Munich and another in Amsterdam in 1941. Mühlmann tapped Weber to be one of his main agents, and as such, Bruno spent most of his time in the Netherlands, Belgium, and northern France, visiting homes that had been recently cleared of their occupants. His task was to survey any remaining artwork and remove the more expensive pieces. Those he deemed suitable for Hitler's planned museum were Sent to Linz, and the rest were sold abroad via local auction houses for foreign currency.

In November 1944, Weber closed his Amsterdam and Berlin galleries and moved his entire operation to Munich. *The timing can't be a coincidence,* Zelda thought.

She closed the folders of information and meditated on the ramifications of her discoveries. She'd come further than Vincent expected her to, yet they still had a long road to go. At least Bruno Weber's gallery gave them a starting point. Although they still didn't know whether Bruno ever had the Vermeer in his possession, there was a significant chance that he was the one who removed it from Roelf's family home and either sent it off to Linz or brokered its sale.

Vincent had at least one solid lead to check out—whenever he had time to do so. The next step would be to follow up with the current owner of the Neue Gallery and see whether they still had access to the gallery's wartime archives.

Zelda wondered whether the paperwork concerning Roelf's artwork still existed or whether it had already been destroyed. Even if they did track it down, would the gallery's current owner cooperate with Vincent? Or would they see him to the door as soon as they realized her boss was implying that the gallery's former owner was associated with the Nazis? But if the gallery had been taken over by a third party, Vincent might get lucky and find a sympathetic ear. Right now, they had little choice. Weber's records were their only hope of finding out more about the confiscation of Roelf's paintings and, hopefully, the Vermeer's current location.

It was too bad she hadn't found any mention of the missing Vermeer in the archives. She had hoped it was sold via Van Marle & Bignell at the same auction, but she could find no listing for it. And Zelda knew from her art history classes that Vermeer was an artist Hitler greatly admired. It should have been earmarked for the Führermuseum in Linz.

After she turned in the archival materials, she slowly walked back to the train station. Considering Vincent had not really expected her to find anything useful, she considered her day of research a success.

When the train arrived, Zelda resolved to type up an email to Vincent and then forget the painting for now. Her parents were due to arrive tomorrow, and ensuring they had a memorable vacation had to be her primary concern. The Vermeer would have to wait.

6

The Golden Quadrangle

Kurt Weber bent over his desk, studying the inventory lists of the paintings hidden away in Stuttgart and Mannheim. He hadn't looked through his father's ledgers in over a decade, and the sheer number was overwhelming.

After he had been released from prison, his dad would often visit his two homes outside of Munich so that he could be with his artwork. Their walls were covered from floor to ceiling with masterpieces that Bruno couldn't stand to be away from for too long.

It was not Bruno's fault that he had been caught selling a forgery. How could he have known that some of the paintings he had saved from Hitler's grasp were, in fact, copies? If that German politician hadn't decided that crucifying Bruno was better than being branded a war profiteer in the press, no one would have been the wiser. By playing dumb and shifting the blame back to Kurt's father, the buyer saved his political career and destroyed the elder Weber's life.

Kurt, on the other hand, frequently made an excuse not to join his father on those pilgrimages. He had always had trouble reconciling Bruno's words with his actions and did his utmost to keep his distance from the collection. After his father had passed, Kurt crated it up, had a state-of-the-art security system installed, and then let it be. Saving the artwork from the Nazis had been the thing Bruno was most proud of, yet his father never made clear what he had hoped would happen to the collection once he was gone. Since Kurt never did figure out how to best deal with this legacy, he chose avoidance over action.

During the war, Kurt's father was an agent of the Mühlmann Agency. Bruno had always said that he relished his work—at least, initially. Hitler's dream of opening a new world-class museum to rival the Louvre was intoxicating, and the elder Weber had been proud to be chosen for the task. It was every art lover's dream.

But as the war dragged on and Bruno was confronted head-on with the human toll, he became increasingly sickened by Hitler's policies. More often, he was called in to confiscate artwork as the families were being arrested, instead of days later. He always said the screams and cries of those taken away by the Gestapo were permanently etched into his memory. The only form of resistance available to him was saving as many paintings as he could from Hitler's grasp. Instead of turning all of the masterpieces over to the Mühlmann Agency, Bruno had kept many of them hidden away, along with ledgers documenting their ownership.

However, after the war ended, Bruno lied about having it. When he was questioned by the Allies about the artwork he had confiscated for the Mühlmann Agency, Bruno swore under oath that he had turned in everything that he had confiscated. It took Kurt many years to understand his father's decision to keep silent. Only after a long night of drinking did his father explain why. During the war, Bruno had saved the art from being sold, burned, or taken as a war trophy by both the Nazis and Red Army. Bruno had gone through so much to save it, he simply couldn't let it go. Instead of returning it, he created two private galleries in his summer homes, their only public other members of the Network.

But after Bruno died, Kurt didn't dare to return the artwork either. Saving it had been his father's proudest moment, and seeing the hundreds of families reunited with their treasures should have been the crowning glory. But how could Kurt explain away the fifty-six pieces his father had sold at a significant profit? There was bound to be a nosy journalist who puzzled that out. Despite Bruno's claims to the contrary, his father was no angel. He had benefited from the sales of the same pieces he swore he was saving, in order to enjoy a luxurious lifestyle.

Gunther's final plea resounded in his mind: *It's not too late to return the artwork. It will never be too late.*

He was right. Holding onto the artwork was a choice, one that could always be reversed. When Kurt learned that Gunther's car had been found at the bottom of a deep ravine the morning after the Network's last meeting, he was confident Max was behind it. How could he be so cruel to Gunther's wife and children, orphaned over artwork Gunther should not have been privy to in the first place? That was Kurt's watershed moment. Max thought that by silencing Gunther, he would quiet any budding resistance within the Network. Kurt was already facing imminent death, so Max couldn't do anything to him that nature wasn't going to do soon enough. This was his chance to set things right.

Kurt had thought long and hard about how to go about the restitution. As much as he would love to announce the collection's existence at a dramatic press conference, his life would be worthless the second he appeared onscreen. Too many prominent German, Swiss, and Austrian citizens were involved in the Network. If the police didn't first place him in protective custody, he would be murdered within hours. But he didn't want to spend the last of his days in a safe house.

There must be another way, he thought.

But how? His choices were limited. In contrast to Gunther's father, Bruno had told him everything about the Network, patiently answering questions about all aspects of its operations. His dad even shared his "black book" with him, a small notebook containing all the names and addresses of the people Bruno had taken artwork from as an agent of the Mühlmann Agency. Kurt had saved it in case the right opportunity to use it ever arose.

Giving that book to the proper authorities might have been enough to accomplish his goals. But the world needed to know that this was not exclusively a German problem—that it was farther reaching. The Network extended throughout Bavaria, Austria, Switzerland, and Lichtenstein, a region some referred to as the Golden Quadrangle. There were enough dealers and auction houses out there still willing to sell their undocumented works and buyers eager to purchase works unavailable to the average art lover.

Kurt stared at the portrait of a dark-haired beauty hanging across from his desk, the only painting from his father's collection hanging in his apartment. The rendering of the woman's astonished expression, her lush curls, and the large ruby pendant hanging around her neck was exquisite. To think this small portrait was nothing more than a marketing tool to show off the artist's talents to potential customers! It was almost absurd to think that artists such as Johannes Vermeer had been forced to scrounge for sponsors and patrons.

As his gaze danced over the fine details, he wondered who it belonged to last. Did its rightful owner also experience a soothing calm whenever he or she had gazed at this gem of a painting? He had never considered the specific details of its provenance before now. Perhaps, subconsciously, he had never wanted to know. It was time to rectify that situation.

7

A Half-Century of Life

Vincent de Graaf cursed the rainstorm hindering his view. From the confines of his rented sedan, it was almost impossible to clearly see the home that his nineteen-year-old suspect was supposedly staying in. Despite several recent sightings by his informants, Vincent had yet to lay eyes on the young man.

He outed his frustrations by bashing his fist against the heater, cursing it to work. *What a long day*, he thought. He had spent most of the afternoon and evening cooped up in this rental car, and so far, he had nothing to show for it.

Vincent was reasonably certain the young man was involved in the theft of several sculptures from a local celebrity's mansion last month. Unfortunately, the boy's mobster uncle made certain no one dared to confirm Vincent's suspicions. In reality, he was more interested in who the boy was working for than prosecuting him. His suspect was young enough that he might accidentally let a clue slip out about his employer—if they ever had a chance to speak. But first, Vincent had to locate the boy.

He was delighted yet surprised when one of his Croatian contacts called to say that the young man had been spotted at his mother's place several times this past week, which was why Vincent had hopped on the next flight to Split as soon as he received the message. Theresa had not been happy with his sudden departure, but Vincent knew he had to do all he could to catch this kid before he disappeared again. For the sake of his business's survival, he needed a win—and fast. Since opening his new office in Split, he had not solved a single case.

As he stared out through the water-covered windows, Vincent contemplated the same question he had been meditating on for the past two hours. Had he tempted fate by opening this Croatian office?

A year ago, opening a second branch seemed like a great idea. So much of the artwork he was paid to search for was recovered in Eastern Europe that he figured being there when the thefts happened would give him a leg up on his competition. But getting his office in Split off the ground had been a struggle, to say the least. His local contacts were surprisingly reluctant to share information as freely as they had when Vincent was based exclusively in Amsterdam. Were they worried about repercussions from those they were informing on? It was proving difficult to meet up with his sources anonymously now that he was based in Split. Too many of those he was investigating knew what he looked like and what his patterns and habits were. If things didn't improve soon, he would need to seriously re-evaluate whether he would keep this office open.

Vincent picked up his phone and opened the birthday ecard from his wife. She had emailed it to him at four in the morning, moments before her flight to Sint Maarten departed. As its merry jingle played, Vincent sighed. Fifty years old. Being cooped up in a car alone and on a stakeout was not how he had envisioned celebrating a half-century of life.

He missed Theresa so much that it hurt. He had hoped she would have relocated to Split by now. With their hectic schedules, they had only seen each other a few days a month, despite living in the same house. He honestly hadn't thought this move would have affected their relationship as much as it had. How wrong he was. Those few hours together were more precious than he'd realized.

In the beginning, Theresa had been as gung-ho as he was about this move. She even talked about transferring her home base to Split so they could see each other during her day-long layovers. As the senior flight attendant, she had the freedom to do so. But after her third visit, Theresa had made it clear that she would not be submitting the request to her employer. Her home, family, and friends were in Amsterdam, and she just couldn't leave them behind.

At first, he didn't understand her sudden change of heart and figured she just needed more time to fall in love with Croatia. It took him days to realize that there was probably another reason she was not enamored with it. When she had taken time off to be with him in Split, he was out on assignment for most of her visits, leaving her alone in his tiny apartment in a city she didn't know.

No wonder she hated it here, he thought to himself, feeling stupid that he hadn't put two and two together earlier.

Still, he could hardly believe that she had decided to work instead of spending this weekend with him. It was his fiftieth, after all. When she'd told him that she was scheduled to fly to Sint Maarten the morning of his birthday, he had flippantly said that he didn't care. He had to work, so she could do what she wanted.

He hated himself for treating her so callously. What was happening to them? They never fought or played mind games. Was this the end of twenty-three beautiful years? Or did they both need space to deal with the transition in their own way? He hoped that it was the latter.

It was probably better that she had not come down to Croatia this weekend, Vincent realized. He wouldn't have had time for her this trip, either, which would have made things infinitely worse.

I really need to take time off work and whisk her off her feet.

The tip-tap dance of rain on the roof was lessening. When Vincent looked toward the house, he could now see that the same lights were on in the same rooms as they had been two hours ago.

Vincent's bladder was about to burst. He'd stepped out to urinate behind a shrub when a car pulled into the driveway he was watching. His suspect stepped out of the passenger's side and waved at Vincent as he walked to his mother's front door. Vincent zipped up his fly and started to run across the street when the driver's door opened. Out stepped the young man's uncle, a thick-necked Croatian gangster with a gun strapped to his side. He also held up his hand in greeting and laughed.

He glared at the men yet waved back. According to his contact, the suspect had been inside the house when Vincent had parked across the street. So either his contact lied, or the kid had seen him watching the house and snuck out the back. Either way, it was clear now that his suspect and uncle knew Vincent was onto them. And his uncle's presence ensured that he would not be able to get near enough to the boy to have a normal conversation.

He got back in his rental car and pounded on the steering wheel in frustration. Nothing was working out how he had hoped.

8

Kurt's Plan

Kurt Weber sat at his desk, gazing up at the Vermeer. Was its rightful owner still alive to claim it? Kurt would probably never know. With the rate the cancer was eating away at his organs, he would be dead before the year's end.

His plan was simple. After much rumination, he had decided on a two-pronged approach. Though most of those he wished to implicate were based in Munich, the world needed to know that this problem extended far beyond Bavaria. For that reason, in the first phase of his plan, he chose to target three Swiss dealers he had worked with in the past.

Setting up the Swiss dealers first would also solve a more pressing problem—his shortage of cash. The money he would make by selling nine of his paintings to the corrupt dealers would be more than enough to fund his initial journey. Things would have been so much easier if one of his friends had agreed to buy out his legitimate stock. He had already contacted several and received lukewarm reactions. He even lied and said he was trying to raise money for an experimental treatment, hoping their sympathy would outweigh their rationality, but alas, there were no takers. He couldn't blame them, really. He had ignored his gallery for so long that the artwork hanging in it was virtually worthless.

The second part of his plan required more preparation. He had already begun writing a detailed letter to the German Advisory Commission, explaining what his father had done and why. Instead of listing all the pieces by their title, he would point the authorities to his father's ledgers, which he planned to leave behind with the artwork. Where, exactly, he had yet to work out.

The next step was adding the names of those he had worked with in Germany, Switzerland, Lichtenstein, and Austria. To truly dismantle the Network, he would need to name those whom he had worked closely with. It was turning into quite a long list. Then again, this Network had existed for three generations, and Kurt knew several important families were involved. His letter implicating them of knowingly trading in looted artwork would have enormous repercussions.

Once this letter was in the hands of the media, he wouldn't be safe in Munich or probably Europe for that matter—too many active players in the Network would seek revenge. Which was why he had already made plans to ensure that he would be in sunny Indonesia before the authorities had the chance to sort through his father's looted artwork or interview those on his list. Bali seemed like a great place to spend the rest of his days.

A hard knock on his door broke Kurt's train of thought. He slipped the letter between the blotter and the desk's mahogany surface before rising. He didn't want anyone to see it until he was ready to send it. As he walked through the living room, he paused to warm his hands at the fireplace, full of broken frames he had found at the back of a closet. When the pounding resumed, Kurt grumbled, "I'm coming," while slowly descending the two flights of steep stairs to his front door. When he looked through the peephole, he cursed silently.

"Hello, Brigitte," Kurt said as he let his visitor inside.

Despite her young age, Brigitte was one of the most serious, businesslike people Kurt had ever had the displeasure of meeting. There was simply nothing positive, warm, or friendly about her. She reminded Kurt of her mother and grandmother before her; both had proved that women could be as heartless and cruel as any man.

Brigitte's grandmother and Max's grandfather had founded the original Network. Both were respectable art dealers in the 1930s who, after the war broke out, wormed their way into Hitler's inner circle. Brigitte's grandmother claimed it was a way to survive. But Bruno had worked closely with them both, and from what he told his son, the Network's founders had not had trouble mingling with the Nazi elite.

Max and Brigitte saw their grandparents as heroes who outsmarted the Third Reich and Allies, which was also why they regarded the leadership roles within the Network as their birthright. In their minds, the artwork had only survived the war thanks to their ancestors' deception, which meant they deserved it more than their rightful owners. To Kurt, Brigitte and Max embodied all of the reasons why it was time to roll this Network up for good.

Brigitte walked into his living room, then turned on her heels to face him. "My condolences. I hear you're dying."

Kurt sank into his couch, in shock. There was only one way Brigitte could have found out about his medical condition—his supposed friends snitched on him. He had only asked a few older dealers he had known for decades, ones he thought would be loyal enough to keep Kurt's request to buy out his gallery, and the reason for it, a secret. He had been foolish to think he was being discreet; too many of his supposed friends relied on the Network for their livelihood.

Kurt was glad he had not dared broach the topic of restitution with any of them. If Max or Brigitte caught wind of what he was doing, he wouldn't survive the day.

Kurt coughed. "Yes, well, if this new treatment works, I'll be around a while longer."

Brigitte examined him closely. "Is that why you are trying to sell your gallery's stock—to pay for medical treatment?"

"Yes, it's an experimental transfusion—a Swiss discovery. I'm traveling to Zurich next week to meet with the doctors. If they accept me into their program, I'll need all the cash I can get ahold of."

"And your inherited collection?"

"It is safe where it's at."

"Are you certain? If you want to unburden yourself and sell it to me, you know I will be generous."

Sure you will, he thought, *as long as the art stays within the Network.*

"Thanks, but no. The artwork is safe where it's at."

"Let me know if you change your mind." Brigitte stood. "When are you going to Zurich?"

"Thursday morning."

"Good luck," she said, her voice cheerless.

"Thanks."

After Brigitte left, Kurt leaned heavily against the door until his blood pressure calmed, then slowly climbed back up to his living room where he poured himself a bourbon. As he swirled the brown liquid around in his glass, he wondered how far Brigitte would go to get ahold of his artwork now that she knew he was terminally ill. Given her resources and contacts, it would be easy enough for her to learn the locations of the apartment and house his father had left him. Would she be gutsy enough to break into them and steal the art?

Yes, he thought ruefully, *she would. Drat!* Because of his weakened state, she would not expect him to fight back.

Kurt cursed aloud. To keep his plan on track, he would have to move the paintings to another location before he left for Switzerland. One Brigitte and Max would not be able to easily find. Kurt bowed his head as he studied his drink. *But where?*

9

Jacob Arrives Home

Zelda's fingers flew over the keyboard as she finished typing a short email to Vincent de Graaf summarizing all she had learned about Roelf's painting. Apart from the attached scans, there weren't many facts to relay.

She searched again on Google Earth for the address of Neue Gallery, navigating to the narrow and windy street it was located on, a short distance from the touristic heart of Munich. There appeared to be artwork hanging inside its windows, though the image was far too blurry to see which pieces they were. According to the gallery's sparse website, it was only open by appointment. Zelda wondered whether Bruno Weber's son knew what his father did during the war and how he felt about it. His attitude toward the Nazi regime would probably determine whether they were able to find out more about the five paintings taken from Roelf's family home in 1942.

It almost seemed like fate that Zelda and her parents were headed to Munich after spending the first week of their visit in the Netherlands. She was so tempted to drop by Neue Gallery then, but she was sure her parents would keep her too busy to do so. And she didn't relish being the one to ask the current owner about the gallery's dark past.

Her thoughts turned to her boss. She hoped his new lead was panning out because he badly needed the money and confidence boost. A wave of guilt washed over her when she considered how her quitting would affect his business plans. Yesterday, her former university mentor emailed her about a job vacancy at a soon-to-be-opened museum in Amsterdam, adding that she thought Zelda would be the perfect candidate. When she took a closer look at the job advertisement, Zelda realized it would be a great fit.

Even before her mentor had reached out to her, looking for another job had been on her mind lately. Working for a private detective sounded so glamorous, but it really was not. To make matters worse, Zelda was also wrestling with her conscience. One of the reasons she loved working for a museum was that her research would ultimately help visitors engage more with a particular object or painting. Vincent's clients were wealthy collectors who could acquire whatever they felt like buying, which meant the art she was researching would inevitably end up in someone's private home. Perhaps, one day, the buyer would donate it to a museum or foundation, but the chances were slim. She missed working with public collections and searching through archives with an eye on what a typical visitor would be interested in, not purely when and where a painting changed hands.

As tempting as it was to apply immediately, she owed it to Vincent to discuss the assistant curator position with him first. He had been so kind in hiring her straight out of university, but he must know that she would ultimately want to pursue a career path more in line with her degree. At least, she hoped he would understand.

Until her parents' visit was over, she wouldn't have time to think about work—either for Vincent or someone else. Her parents had never been to Europe before, and she wanted to make the best impression possible. Zelda knew they didn't understand why she had decided to stay in Amsterdam and hoped spending a week here would be enough to convince them that it was a great place for her to settle down. Especially now that Jacob was in her life and seemingly as smitten with Amsterdam as she was.

Zelda bit her lip, hoping her parents approved of her list of things to do while they were in the Netherlands.

Truth be told, she didn't know what they would enjoy doing most while on vacation. Her parents had never been interested in traveling, meaning family vacations were extremely rare. They were happy with their home, garden, friends, and work. Her dad loved being a realtor and had trouble stepping back for a week or two, convinced his competition would get a massive jump on him if he did. Her mom was part of so many committees and charity organizations that she barely had enough time for her work as head librarian of their local branch. Which was why their decision to come to Europe for two full weeks was even more special. Zelda wanted their trip to be unforgettable.

As she reviewed her email to Vincent, she heard the front door click open. Her heart began to race when Jacob called out, "I'm home, babe."

Zelda yelled back, "I'm in the study. Be right there."

She pushed send as Jacob entered the tiny closet—its shelves loaded up with all of their computer and stereo gear—that they jokingly referred to as their home office.

Zelda rose, and they locked in a passionate embrace. She melted as Jacob ran his hand up her shirt, reveling in the feeling of his skin on hers. For the past few months, they had only seen each other during the weekends. However, he was two months away from completing his project in Cologne. Zelda was thrilled to hear he had already lined up a part-time lecturer position at the Open University in Amsterdam. It sounded like a perfect fit for him and, more importantly, would bring him back to Amsterdam. Germany was too far away for the long term.

"Do you have more work to do before your parents arrive?" he asked.

"This was the last of it. I wanted to send Vincent all of the information I discovered about Roelf's paintings while it's still fresh in my mind. I'll probably forget something important if I try to send it in two weeks."

"I think you're right about that. We're going to be pretty busy. It's so special that they want to fly over." He nuzzled her neck.

Zelda was pleased by how happy he was to meet her parents. She responded with a kiss. "It is quite a shock. They've always found an excuse not to visit. Though they still haven't told me why they decided to come over now."

Jacob kept his face hidden in her neck and remained silent. Suspiciously so.

"Wait a second—do you know what's going on?" Zelda pushed him back and raised an eyebrow at him.

Jacob wouldn't meet her gaze, but a grin split his face. "I don't know what you're talking about. Do you have anything new to share about the Vermeer?"

"Hey! No changing the subject! What's going on? Are you all ganging up on me? What have they planned, and why do you know about it and not me?" Zelda tickled his armpits.

"Hey, stop!" Jacob squirmed. "I can't tell you. It's a surprise."

"I hate surprises."

"I know, but I promised your parents. They needed my help to arrange part of it. You'll have to wait for this one. Your parents went to too much trouble, so I can't mess it up for them."

Was it a belated birthday present, Zelda wondered. Or her parents' golden anniversary? Were they considering buying property over here? Or thinking of retiring? Both turned seventy last year, so she wouldn't be surprised if this trip were a test run for an around-the-world cruise or some such thing. If either one of them was ill, her mom would have told her. But what else could it be? There were too many possibilities.

Zelda considered her options. She could tickle the information out of Jacob or respect her parents' wishes and let it go. Considering this was her last chance to be alone with her boyfriend before her parents arrived, she chose the latter.

"Okay, out of parental respect, I'll leave it. For now." She grabbed his hand and led him to their bedroom.

10

Calling in a Favor

Kurt was having trouble getting his heart rate to slow down. He had spent the day crating up the artwork currently stored in Stuttgart and was utterly spent. It had been an extraordinarily long day for even a healthy man, and Kurt looked forward to stretching out on his couch with a glass of bourbon. He still had one more stop before he could go home and truly unwind. Luckily, it would include dessert.

Kurt hated having to ask his best friend for this favor, but he felt as if he had no choice. Brigitte was a vulture already circling, and he didn't trust her to leave his father's artwork alone. Helmut was his only friend that was neither part of the Network nor interested in art. He had to hide his father's paintings somewhere they wouldn't think to look for it, and Helmut's home in Heidelberg, the town they had met in so many years ago, was the perfect place.

They became friends at university during a course in Bavarian culture and had been close ever since. During his sophomore year, Kurt rented one of the rooms in Helmut's spacious family home, situated in the heart of Heidelberg's historical center. After they graduated, they moved back to Munich and shared an apartment until Helmut met the woman he later married.

Kurt chose modern art over ethnography. Helmut spent thirty years as a professor of anthropology, dedicating his life to folks' cultures. He also founded Germany's first intangible culture research center, recording thousands of hours of dances, songs, and crafts demonstrations. Most importantly, Helmut was a staunch advocate of the restitution of ethnographic objects. Kurt knew his friend would stand behind his decision and help as much as he could.

Which was good because there was no one else he could trust with this assignment. Not only did Kurt want to use his friend's home as a storage facility, but he also hoped Helmut would help him ensure that his plan was fully executed. If Kurt was killed before the police responded to his letter, he needed to know there was somebody left in Germany who could alert the media and, if necessary, take them to the artwork. Which meant someone outside of the Network had to be informed about the artwork's history and know where it was being stored.

Kurt rang his friend's doorbell, knowing Helmut was home. He was a creature of habit and would be sitting down to afternoon tea right about now.

He waited patiently for his friend to answer and embraced him warmly once inside.

"Kurt, how are you feeling?" Helmut was the only one who knew the truth about the aggressive nature of his cancer and that the end was near.

"I'm a little worn out."

"I have the perfect remedy," Helmut said as he led his friend into his living room. On the coffee table was a strudel. Helmut grabbed a plate and cut a thick slice for his friend. "Freshly made," he said, automatically adding two dollops of whipped cream to Kurt's serving.

Kurt watched how the cream melted a little and slid off the warm dessert. He breathed in the sweet cinnamon and honey before taking a healthy bite. His stomach murmured in approval.

After Helmut poured Kurt a cup of tea, he scanned his friend's face. "Is there anything I can do for you? You look exhausted."

Kurt would so miss his friend's generosity and kindness. He deeply regretted having to get Helmut involved. Doing so would put his friend's life in danger, but he had to trust someone.

Kurt savored his last bite of strudel before telling his friend everything.

11

Windmills of Zaanse Schans

"Zelda, could you take another picture of us with those in the background?" her mother, Debbie, asked, pointing over her shoulder at a pair of windmills towering over the banks of the River Zaan.

"Say cheese," Zelda said.

Her father, Terry, pulled her mom in close, and both smiled broadly. After she'd taken several shots, her dad said, "Hey, Jacob. Get over here, kid."

"Are you sure?" Jacob asked.

"You're practically family," Zelda's dad said reassuringly, waving him over.

Jacob blushed and did as he asked.

"Okay, Zelda, time to switch," Jacob called out after she had snapped several photos. He exchanged places with his girlfriend so that she also had mementos from her parents' visit.

They were standing on a balcony-like platform skirting around the thatched body of De Kat, the only paint-powder-producing windmill still in operation. From here, they had great views of the cute green wooden houses of Zaandam on the other side of the river, as well as the vast pastureland behind them. They were also at eye level with the massive blades swooshing by, driving the toothed wheels and radars inside that crushed the minerals into paint powder.

The past five days had been a whirlwind of cheese tours, boat trips, fishing villages, wooden shoes, and now windmills. Zelda couldn't have planned a more Dutch experience and was so relieved by how smoothly everything was going. Her parents loved Amsterdam, far more than she expected. Her dad even asked to visit the Rijksmuseum a second time. Zelda was thrilled.

She had saved Zaanse Schans for their last day in the Netherlands, wanting to end their week with a bang. The tiny village, famous for its windmills, was a short drive from Amsterdam. Although Zaanse Schans was one of the more renowned tourist hotspots in the region, Zelda loved it.

She was also pleased to see how well Jacob was getting along with her parents. Because of his rather reserved and analytical nature, Zelda wasn't sure they would take a shine to him. She was so glad they had discovered his warm and charming side. And Zelda was grateful Jacob was so gracious about her parents' quirks. Her mother could not pass a souvenir shop without popping inside, and her father's lifelong career as a realtor meant she had been looking up apartment prices every time they came across a "For Sale" sign.

The more she pondered this surprise they had planned, the more she thought it must have something to do with buying property. Maybe they were considering purchasing a small apartment for her to live in, if only as an investment.

Her mom was unusually quiet today. Zelda figured it was because they were heading to Munich in the morning. Their flight over from Seattle had been extremely turbulent, so Zelda could imagine she wasn't looking forward to flying again.

After they'd descended the steep ladders and were back outside, Zelda's asked, "Pumpkin, could we stop and eat? I'm famished."

She blushed a little at the use of her pet name but said nothing. It was her daddy, after all.

"I saw a couple of cafés next to the parking lot. Why don't we head back and see if they have any of those heavenly pastrami sandwiches," he suggested.

Zelda figured her dad would eat his way through Europe, and so far, she'd been right. He'd eaten raw herring—the Dutch way—explored the extensive menu of fried snacks, and ate more cheese than was good for anyone, let alone an overweight, relatively short man in his early seventies. Just thinking about all the liquors, beers, and wines they'd sampled this week gave her a headache.

After her mother nodded in agreement, they walked over the dike along the River Zaan, then followed a muddy path winding through the tiny village and back to the parking lot. Together, they examined the multilingual menus at the only café with tables available. Sandwiches didn't seem to be on offer, but pancakes were.

"I don't want breakfast," her dad grumbled.

"Pancakes aren't just for breakfast here. Dutch people eat them all day long. They aren't at all what you would get back home. I bet you'll like it."

They ordered pancakes as large as a plate and topped with strips of bacon, pineapple, ham and cheese, apple compote, and a massive amount of syrup and powdered sugar. Despite their size, they were gone in minutes.

"That was delicious. I would never have thought of cooking bacon and cheese into the pancake. Although I still prefer them for breakfast, I'm glad you convinced us." Her dad patted her on the back.

"It's been a real treat getting to know your city, Zelda. What a place. Right, Debbie?" he continued as he threw an arm over her mom's shoulder. "We can see why you love Amsterdam."

Zelda beamed, delighted by his words. "Phew, I am so glad. All I wanted was for you to understand why I want to live here, even if you would not."

"Oh, hon, we completely understand why you want to stay. It's a big city, yet not as hectic as New York or Los Angeles. I think you've made a good choice," her mother reassured her.

Zelda rose and hugged her parents, enormously relieved to hear these words. After she regained control of her emotions, she picked up her backpack and pulled out a thin box as broad as two pieces of paper. "I made you something and figured this was the place to give it to you. It's for both of you, but I'll let Mom do the honors."

She handed the box to her mother and crossed her fingers. She had spent the past month making a special stained-glass window for her parents as a keepsake of their trip. After struggling to come up with an idea, she'd settled for a traditional windmill surrounded by tulips. She was pretty happy with the result of her first figurative project. She only hoped her parents loved it, too.

"Oh, Zelda, it's perfect. And I see why you wanted to give it to us at Zaanse Schans. It's a great way to memorialize our trip," Debbie said, a tear forming in her eye.

After her parents enthused over the window, her mother took her hand. "My dear, we have a surprise for you, too. We've asked Jacob to join us on our trip to Munich. It's been such a pleasure getting to know your boyfriend that we didn't want to leave him behind for the second week of our trip."

Zelda's eyes widened in astonishment. So that was what they had been planning.

"That's wonderfully generous of you!" She kissed Jacob on the cheek. "I've felt so bad about leaving him behind."

Jacob laughed. "It's been difficult not to say anything every time you apologized for going on vacation without me."

Zelda crinkled her nose as a thought struck her. "But aren't you supposed to present your latest findings to the museum's board of directors next week?"

"I've already talked to my boss, and we pushed the meeting to the afternoon so I can take a train back to Cologne from Munich the same morning you and your parents fly back to Amsterdam."

"That's fantastic. Now I understand why you all had to talk this through before you came over. Thanks for including Jacob, Mom and Dad." Zelda lifted her coffee in a toast. "To Munich!"

12

Setting Up the Swiss

Kurt sipped coffee out of a ridiculously small porcelain cup as he gazed out at the snowcapped peaks of the Alps.

Claude peered at him over rimless spectacles. "You're looking poorly."

Kurt chuckled at his old friend's bluntness. Well, "friend" was too strong a word. Their fathers had been good friends. Out of respect, Claude always gave him a slightly higher percentage of the take than usual. However, Kurt had never warmed to the Swiss dealer, who was too reserved and businesslike for his tastes.

Before boarding the train to Zurich, Kurt assembled dossiers about each of the three dealers he would be visiting during this short trip—including the titles of all of the paintings they had taken off his hands in the past twenty years. Kurt was certain the Swiss men had resold them for a generous profit.

Though it wasn't illegal to sell a painting without verifying its provenance, most art lovers considered it to be a moral obligation, especially when an esteemed dealer was involved. Once Kurt's dossier was in the hands of the media, Claude's reputation would suffer, and the major museums on his clientele list would avoid purchasing any pieces from him. That was enough justice for Kurt.

"I've been diagnosed with an aggressive form of lung cancer, which is why I'm here today. The doctors have told me about an experimental treatment that may help. However, it's quite expensive."

"I was wondering why you brought in three paintings this time instead of one. That also explains why you made appointments with Alfred and Rudolf later today."

Kurt blushed. He should have known the three dealers would keep each other informed of any movement within the Network. He shrugged. "I need all the cash I can muster."

His profession as an art dealer made it easier to transport art across borders without raising a customs official's suspicions. Still, nine paintings were as many as he dared transport at one time.

"So, what have you brought me today?" Claude glanced impatiently at the canvas bag on his desk. Kurt had said in an email how many paintings he was bringing, but he had intentionally not mentioned the artists' names.

Kurt carefully unzipped the case and removed works made by Henri Matisse, Emil Nolde, and Ernst Ludwig Kirchner. Kurt knew the dealer would be shocked to see these. Kurt usually only sold works created by the lesser artists in his father's collection, but this time, it was essential to bring in more recognizable painters. Kurt figured it would help simplify the next phase of his plan. He also knew Claude, Alfred, and Rudolf would take more time to find the right buyer for each piece, one willing and able to pay millions for these works. By the time the police received his letter, the artwork would most likely still be in their possession. At least, Kurt hoped so.

The Swiss dealer grunted appreciatively. "Are you certain you want to part with these?"

"Yes. They're not doing me any good in storage, and I want to start the treatment as soon as possible."

Claude considered all three. "Wire transfer or cash?"

"Cash."

Claude blinked rapidly, and Kurt felt as if he were watching a calculator at work.

"Twenty-five?"

Kurt snorted. "I'm no fool. Whoever buys these will pay you a fortune, especially if they know they were looted." *How could the buyer not know?*

thought Kurt as he gazed at the masterfully painted pieces. All three were exquisite examples of these artists' abilities. "Two hundred," Kurt said, chuckling internally when Claude's eyes bugged out.

The Swiss dealer glared at him. "Seventy-five, and that's my final offer."

"Do you have enough cash here?"

"Just."

"Okay. It's a deal."

Claude looked relieved. Kurt knew he should have pushed for more, but he really couldn't be bothered to negotiate further with this twerp. And it was imperative that Claude take all three pieces, if his plan were to work.

Kurt stood and offered his hand. Greed and a desire to have what others could not motivated the dealers and clients working within the Network. He was pleased to see how predictable both could make a man. Completing the first phase of his plan would be easier than he anticipated.

13

Keeping Up Appearances

Kurt opened his front door and breathed a deep sigh of relief. He had made it back to Munich without a whiff of trouble. The ziplock bags and duct tape he had brought along were perfect for attaching the money to his body.

The train ride back also gave him time to polish his letter to the media and police about the Swiss dealers he had just met with. Luckily, his first-class carriage was otherwise empty, giving him the space he needed to consider every detail that should be included in it. He had offered three dealers a trio of paintings each, and all three had accepted, providing him with enough cash to fund years of island living—not that he expected to be around that long. After he mailed this letter, the first phase of his plan would be complete. But before he could do that, he had to ensure the second phase was ready to commence.

He didn't expect the police to immediately react to his email about his Swiss friends trading in looted paintings. But he did expect the media to take more direct action. After all, he was accusing three of Switzerland's most respected art dealers of being war profiteers. Kurt imagined there would be camera crews camped out on their doorsteps as soon as their reporters had a chance to review the information he was providing.

Kurt didn't care how long it took the police or media to react so long as he was already out of Munich when they did. The last thing he wanted was to be interviewed in connection with this case—by either party. To slow down their cyberdetectives, Kurt had already located an internet café without a working security system on the outskirts of the city. He would create a new email account and type the letter in there. Still, he wouldn't be surprised if cameras placed in neighboring streets would capture his image, regardless.

Luckily, Helmut had helped him move the art to Heidelberg before he left for Zurich. They had even enjoyed a lovely afternoon together, reminiscing about their university days while walking around their old stomping grounds. Taking the funicular railway to the top of the Königstuhl was a highlight of their trip—oh, how he missed the magnificent views from that mountaintop.

Kurt set his suitcase down and waddled to his bedroom, where he quickly undressed before carefully removing the duct tape holding wads of cash to his legs and back. The tape was so sweaty that it loosened easily. Once his body was free from the two hundred and sixty thousand euros in cash, he took a long shower, scrubbing the sticky residue from his skin.

The warm water set his thoughts drifting. It was still early morning. He could send the email, then stop by Helmut's for lunch after. That gave him the afternoon to pack up his luggage and arrange for an evening taxi ride to Heidelberg. He wanted to visit his artwork one more time before he left Germany forever. From there, he could take a shuttle bus to Frankfurt Airport.

Heidelberg had a plethora of internet cafés from which he could send his second email before leaving town. It would probably be smarter to send it from there, rather than from the airport, he realized, in case the police could trace his electronic message to the café from which he had sent it. The second email was his swan song. It would certainly ruin the lives of all involved and tarnish their family names forever. Kurt thought about his fellow members, their partners, and their children. It pained him to hurt them, but he felt as if he had no choice. It was long past time to roll up the Network and return the artwork to the rightful owners' heirs.

Kurt had inherited almost four hundred prints and paintings from his father; he could only imagine what the other thirteen members possessed. Most of it was hidden away in storage units and second homes, only to be pulled out of their protective crates when those responsible for them needed cash. Gunther was right; the current generation would never voluntarily return the art. As long as there were auction houses, collectors, and art dealers willing to look the other way, the paintings were far too valuable to simply give back.

"Hypocrite," he mumbled into the foggy mirror as he dried off. Over the years, he had sold several prints and a handful of paintings whenever he needed a cash injection. Kurt had tried to make his own way in the world, but the gallery was never as successful as he'd hoped it would be. He simply didn't have the eye for art that his father did. Instead, he had relied on the looted collection to support him during the leaner months.

Shame coursed through his body. That reliance was the reason he had never returned the paintings to their rightful owners. His father's black book provided all the information he needed to trace the owners of each piece. If only he had taken the time to do so. Now it was a burden for another. He didn't have enough time left on the planet to do it all, and these pieces needed to go home. Better late than never, he reckoned, hoping history would be kind to him—and that he could stay one step ahead of the Network long enough to die a natural death.

Kurt finished drying himself and pulled on his best suit. He was always careful to dress immaculately and didn't want his neighbors to suspect anything was amiss. The last thing he did was slip the letter about the Swiss dealers, along with the draft he was writing to the restitution committee, into his coat pocket. He wanted to show the second one to Helmut later and discuss the wording as well as when he should send it.

It was the timing that worried him most. So many powerful people were named in his letter that he was certain as soon as that news hit, he would be a marked man. Kurt leaned against his bedroom wall and took a deep breath. If everything went according to plan, by the time the discovery of the looted art hit the news, he should be flying over the Indian Ocean.

14

Exploring Munich

"Isn't that incredible," Debbie whispered.

Zelda stood between her parents and boyfriend in the Marienplatz, gazing up in wonder at the show taking place in the Rathaus's imposing tower. Munich's world-famous Rathaus-Glockenspiel had just begun. They were all enthralled by the ancient figures' costumes as they danced around the medieval tower in time to a tinkling melody. Zelda's favorite was the life-sized knights on horseback, re-enacting a joust held in honor of Duke Wilhelm V's marriage.

"It truly is," Zelda responded.

The first half of their trip to Munich had gone by so quickly that Zelda could hardly believe they were only here for three more days. She'd had reservations about visiting here when her parents first suggested it, but their friends were right; the Bavarian city was beautiful, the locals exceedingly friendly, and the food delicious. The sturdy stone buildings, heavily decorated with massive swirls and carved decorations or painted designs, were whimsical and colorful. Wide boulevards connected by small curvy streets wound through the vast heart of the city like a river's many tributaries.

They had visited several palaces and churches in the city center, including the massive Munich Residence, the former royal palace of the Wittelsbach monarchs of Bavaria. Markets, beer gardens, and cute souvenir shops kept them busy between their cultural outings.

If only Mom could walk by a shop without looking inside, we would have seen more, Zelda thought. Her father was already laden with gifts, and it was just noon.

As the figures' dancing slowed, a golden rooster at the top of the Glockenspiel quietly chirped three times, marking the end of the spectacle.

The crowd, gathered around the base of the tower, clapped heartily before dispersing.

"Pumpkin, is that beer garden nearby? Or do we need to find a bus?" her dad asked.

"I don't know if the Hofbräuhaus is close by or not. Let me take a look." Zelda dutifully pulled out a map and oriented herself.

"It should be just behind the Marienplatz."

Her father looked at her blankly.

"That is where we are standing now. I think if we walk past the toy museum over there, we should be there in a few minutes. I can help you carry some bags if you want."

"No, I'm balanced right now. If you remove one, I might topple over."

The many bags her father was holding were filled with gifts for all of their friends back home. *At least they will get a prize for suffering through all the photos,* she thought. Her parents had taken hundreds since they had arrived.

Zelda had just started leading them past the toy museum toward a church on the backside of Marienplatz when a large open-air market on their right caught her mother's eye.

Zelda sighed. Sensing her irritation, Jacob squeezed her hand tight and smiled. "She must have forgotten to buy gifts for her neighbor's sister's book club," he whispered in her ear, getting a giggle out of Zelda.

They dutifully followed her parents around the market as her mother poked her head into each of the many arts and crafts booths. After they'd made a complete round, Zelda's parents disappeared into a shop on a quiet corner just behind the market. By the time she and Jacob caught up with them, Zelda's mother already had a wooden candle holder in her hand and was negotiating. For some reason, her mother tried to barter for every purchase she made. At first, Zelda was mortified, yet to her surprise, most shopkeepers played along and gave her mother substantial discounts. Zelda figured it was due to the sheer number of purchases she made. Her mom must have bought gifts for every neighbor, co-worker, grocery clerk, garbage man, and volunteer friend she knew. Zelda wondered whether they would have to purchase another piece of luggage to get it all home.

Instead of heading inside, Zelda and Jacob stood outside the small shop, hand in hand, and watched through the window as Debbie worked her magic.

"Do you know how close we are to the Hofbräuhaus? I wouldn't mind eating soon," Jacob asked, keeping his voice low. Even though her parents were inside the shop, he didn't want to risk offending them. Zelda was amazed by how respectful he had been this entire trip.

"Let me check." Zelda unwound her arm from his and grabbed her map. While she tried to locate their exact position, a nearby street name drew her attention.

"Hey, the Neue Gallery is on the Hackenstrasse. According to this map, it's only a few blocks away, though in the wrong direction from the Hofbräuhaus. Do you think we could talk my parents into taking a detour after lunch? I've been reading so much about it that I'd love to see it with my own eyes."

Jacob grimaced. "I don't think your parents would be interested in checking out an art gallery. Besides, if there are any souvenir shops on that street, we might not make it there until after it closes."

Zelda bit her lip. "You're right. Going together is a horrible idea."

They looked inside the shop. Zelda's mother had both hands full, and the salesman was grabbing a ladder to reach a higher shelf. Her father was leaning against the counter, his eyes partially closed. "It looks like Mom is going to be a while longer. Darling, would you mind terribly if I popped by the gallery to see if it's even open? If it's not, the current residents might know what happened to it. It would save Vincent a trip to Munich, especially if the gallery doesn't exist anymore."

Jacob's eyebrows creased together. "What about your parents?"

"Would you mind keeping an eye on them for a few minutes? I think they would panic if we left them alone. And I'm fairly certain they would not be able to find the beer garden or hotel on their own." Zelda had noticed that her parents were having a hard time orienting themselves in these maze-like streets and neighborhoods.

She looked around and pointed to a small café just behind them. "If Mom gets done before I return, why don't I meet you there? When I get back, we can walk to the Hofbräuhaus together."

Jacob nodded in agreement. "That sounds like a good idea."

Zelda took his hands and kissed his fingertips, thrilled she had such a supportive boyfriend. "I promise to be back within twenty minutes and not a second longer. If I can't find the gallery by then, it's Vincent's problem. Either way, I owe you big-time."

Jacob kissed her lightly on the lips and whispered, "I can think of a few ways you could pay me back."

Zelda reddened and nuzzled his cheek, well aware that her parents could see them through the shop's window. "We'll have to discuss your payment tonight. But for now, I am going to check out the gallery while Mom is still distracted. See you in a few minutes."

15

Visiting the Neue Gallery

Zelda speed-walked up the Hackenstrasse, scanning the house numbers without breaking stride. It was a short road connecting two busy boulevards, made narrow by the cars parked on both sides. Soon, she was standing in front of the Neue Gallery. It had the same logo and name as the original Amsterdam location and appeared to be open for business. When Zelda walked up to the entrance, she noticed a small sign taped to the inside of the door. In German and English, it read, "Open by Appointment Only." The telephone number was also listed.

"Well, I'll be," she muttered, amazed that it was still in operation. Vincent would be pleased to know that. She cupped her hands against the window to see inside better. A few landscapes were hanging in the first room, but it looked as if the rest of the space was empty. Maybe she was too optimistic. Was the gallery really open, or had Kurt Weber passed on and no one had bothered to take down the sign?

There's one way to find out, Zelda thought as she pulled out her phone and dialed. She knew Vincent wanted to conduct any interviews, but she also knew he felt this search was hopeless. He was convinced that even if they did find the gallery, the current owner probably wouldn't be keen to share documentation implicating their business in the selling of Nazi-looted artwork.

But Zelda was the one who had done all the research into Bruno Weber and his gallery, and she was convinced a clue to the Vermeer's location could be found in his paperwork. As the phone rang, she hoped for an unwitting assistant or a new owner who wasn't afraid to confront the past.

On the tenth ring, a deep, guttural voice answered, "*Guten tag*, Kurt Weber speaking."

Zelda's eyes widened in shock. After reading so much about his father, she could hardly believe she had Kurt Weber on the phone. "Hello, sir. My name is Zelda Richardson. I am trying to locate the owner of Neue Gallery. Are you, by chance, him? Or do you know where I could find him?"

"Yes, I am the owner. How can I help you?" His breathing was ragged, as if he had rushed to answer the phone and overexerted himself.

"Excellent. I work for a Dutch private investigator who is trying to verify the provenance of a painting. The seller claims to have bought it from your gallery several years ago but doesn't have the title transfer. I hoped you might still have a copy of it or a ledger mentioning the sale. I am standing outside your gallery now. Are you available to chat? I promise not to take up much of your time, sir." Zelda knew she was crossing a line, but her adrenaline was already pumping. While she was here, she might as well save Vincent the trouble of finding out where the archives were held—if they even existed. If Weber didn't have them, she would be saving Vincent a trip to Munich.

Silence met her request, and Zelda shivered as the wind kicked up. She hoped he would at least hear her out, but it looked as if he wasn't going to let her inside. She started to back away, when Kurt Weber answered, "One moment," then the line went dead. Zelda could hear heavy footsteps approaching before the gallery door opened.

"Your timing is impeccable. I just returned home." He stepped aside to let her pass. Kurt Weber was a short, barrel-chested man in his late sixties with a few wisps of gray still hanging onto the top of his head. His gaunt face was flushed as if he'd been exerting himself far too much, and based on his grayish skin and watery eyes, he appeared to be quite ill. He was well-dressed but sweaty with dark circles under his eyes, and despite his girth, his suit hung loose, as if he'd recently lost weight.

Zelda ducked to miss hitting her head on the gallery's low threshold. The walls were covered with dark wood panels, and tiny spotlights were placed above the few paintings currently hanging in the gallery. Zelda's footsteps disappeared into the thick carpet with an intricate gold pattern woven into plush red. She glanced dutifully at the art hanging in the small space. It was a mix of abstract landscapes and still lifes—none of which Zelda would have called extraordinary.

"Mr. Weber, thank you for seeing me. You have a lovely gallery."

Kurt Weber rubbed his hands together briskly. The open door brought in the cold. "Thank you, madam. Would you care to warm up with a coffee or tea?"

"Tea would be lovely."

"Why don't we go upstairs to my kitchen? We can talk while the kettle boils."

He led Zelda to a staircase at the back of the gallery, moving slowly as if every step took effort. As she followed him up the stairwell, she hoped Vincent would understand why she was having tea with this art dealer. If Weber had the paperwork they sought, she would call Vincent tonight and let him handle the rest. If he didn't, they were back to square one.

The steep staircase brought them into a small yet cozy living room where most of the furniture was antique, though well-worn. It didn't look like Kurt had enough cash to get the chairs reupholstered or repair the tattered oriental rugs.

He walked through to a tiny kitchen, and Zelda stood in the doorway while he set the kettle. "So your client wishes to buy a painting that the current owner said was purchased from Neue Gallery. Why do you need to verify it? Does the buyer suspect it is a forgery?"

"To be honest," Zelda stammered, unsure how much she should tell him, "I'm not really verifying a painting's provenance but trying to find a piece lost long ago. We have reason to believe that the painting passed through your Amsterdam gallery in 1942. My boss, a private detective named Vincent de Graaf, was planning on contacting you next week. My family and I are here on vacation, and when I noticed we were close to your gallery, I thought I would see if you still had the business ledgers from the 1940s."

Kurt's eyes widened. He was obviously startled by the date. "Yes, well, I do still have our old paperwork tucked away in our storage unit, from my father's time as owner. Tell me more about the painting you are investigating—what is the title and artist's name?"

The kettle boiled, drawing Kurt away, so Zelda used the moment to collect her thoughts.

Kurt handed her a cup of hot water and a box filled with tea bags.

"I know this is going to sound crazy, but it is a portrait by Johannes Vermeer."

Kurt swore in German and leaned heavily against the wall, almost tipping over his tea mug in the process. He paled so rapidly, Zelda was afraid he was having a heart attack. "I need to sit down," he whispered.

Zelda took his elbow and helped him to his couch. After he was settled, he asked, "Why do you think Neue Gallery sold it?"

"I don't know that your gallery did. In the National Archives in The Hague, I found an auction catalog that shows that Bruno Weber brought four paintings to Van Marle & Bignell auction house in The Hague in 1942. These four paintings were taken from my client's family home in May of that year, along with a portrait by Vermeer that has since disappeared. Based on the documentation we found, we believe Bruno Weber confiscated all five paintings from their home. But what happened to the Vermeer afterwards is still a mystery. It is a long shot, but we hoped that Weber had made some sort of notation about what had happened to it. I truly do not want to offend you by dredging up the past, but this is the first solid lead we have found. We just wanted to know if perhaps your documentation could help us continue to trace its current whereabouts."

When she noticed Kurt shifting uncomfortably in his seat, Zelda added, "Nobody will be prosecuting anybody about this. We really don't care how it came into your father's possession. Our client just wants to know what happened to his mother's painting."

"And why does your client want to find it? To sell it at auction?" The man's voice was filled with bitterness.

"No, nothing like that. From what I understand, he was a successful film producer in America before retiring and is wealthy. His parents were killed in a concentration camp, and all that they owned was confiscated or sold. Their art collection is all that's left, but most of it disappeared during the war. All of the pieces his lawyers have recovered have been immediately lent to public museums so that everyone can enjoy them. It's really not about the money," Zelda said firmly. She knew many heirs sold the reclaimed artwork, often out of necessity. The legal fees involved in a restitution claim were often astronomical.

The man stared at her with watery eyes, holding her gaze as he examined her soul. At least that was what it felt like he was doing.

"What is his family name?"

"The artwork was taken from Ruth and Siegfried Konig, but they were sent to concentration camps and didn't survive the war. The claimant is their son, Roelf."

"Hmm, I don't know this name. Can you describe their Vermeer to me?"

"It's a small portrait of a dark-haired young woman wearing an off-the-shoulder dress and a large ruby pendant around her neck."

The older man gaped. Zelda felt a tinge of awe. *My God, could he really know what happened to the Vermeer?* She dared not speak lest she break his train of thought.

"I know this painting quite well. I will have to check my father's records to see how he acquired it, and from whom."

Zelda's heart skipped a beat. "Sir, are you telling me that you know where the Vermeer is?"

"Yes, I do. It is hanging in my study. I didn't know the owners were murdered. My father didn't note that kind of information in his ledgers. If you bring me proof of this man's ownership, I will return it to Konig's son."

"What? Are you serious?" Zelda sank into a chair, completely overwhelmed with joy—until reality kicked in. Why would this art dealer give a painting worth millions to a virtual stranger? Was this a vicious trick he was trying to play on a Nazi victim? Would that make it a hate crime? She couldn't tell Huub or Vincent about the Vermeer unless she was certain it was really here. Neither man would believe her otherwise.

"From what I understand, Roelf has been searching for this painting for decades. I can't tell him you have it unless I see it for myself. It would be too cruel."

Kurt nodded solemnly. "I understand your skepticism." He looked into his teacup as he continued. "I just found out that I am dying. I have no heirs, meaning there is no one left to care for the paintings. If you had come by a month earlier, I would not have let you inside. As I said earlier, your timing is impeccable," he said with a half smile. "Please follow me."

At the end of the hallway was his study, complete with a desk, a bookshelf, and two comfortable-looking chairs. The only window's shade was drawn. Zelda thought that was strange until she looked to where the sunlight would land. On that wall hung an oil painting not much larger than a sheet of paper. A gorgeous young woman looked at her in astonishment, as if Zelda had interrupted her dressing. A tortoiseshell comb held her dark hair off her face, though a few curly strands had fallen loose, framing her neck. The dark yellows and oranges of the colorful dress complemented the blood-red ruby hanging on a pendant around her neck. The way Vermeer painted the young woman, it seemed as if she could jump out of the portrait and run away.

"Holy s…" Zelda swallowed her words and turned to her host. "How? Why?"

"My father was an agent for the Mühlmann Agency. Have you heard of them?"

"Yes, sir, I have," Zelda murmured.

"Then you know how they acquired so many paintings and sculptures," Kurt said. "My father worked for them during the war and was responsible for selling off confiscated paintings to buyers abroad. He couldn't stand to see so many masterpieces taken from their rightful owners and sold to strengthen the Nazi war machine. So he began hiding some of them away instead of turning all of them over to Mühlmann. He saved hundreds of paintings. Unfortunately, when the war ended, he kept them secreted away instead of turning them over to the Allies. And after he died, they passed to me."

Zelda felt the hairs rise on the back of her neck. "Why are you telling me all of this? Aren't you afraid I will tell the police?" Zelda began worrying this was some sort of sick setup.

Kurt looked at her with such a pained expression, as if she had deeply offended him. She couldn't tell why, but her nervousness lessened.

"I do not have long to live. I am getting ready to turn over the entire collection to the German authorities so that they can return these paintings to their rightful owners. If you want the Vermeer but don't want to deal with German bureaucracy, please bring Roelf's proof of ownership back here before six o'clock tonight," he said. "Now, if you will excuse me, I need to finish packing. I wish to spend my last days with my loved ones."

Zelda was awash with emotions. She let Kurt escort her downstairs to his apartment's front door.

As he opened it, Zelda pulled one of Vincent's business cards out of her purse and scribbled her phone number on the back. "If there are any changes, could you please give me a call?"

Kurt pocketed the card. "Remember, be back before six," he said, then closed the door firmly.

Zelda couldn't believe it. "Yes!" she cried out, giggling as she pulled out her phone to call Vincent. He was never going to believe this.

16

Skeptical Hope

"Huub, it's no joke. He showed me the painting and told me how his father acquired it," Zelda said while walking up a wide boulevard busy with shoppers and tourists heading to and from the city center.

Zelda was still in shock at her discovery and the willingness of Kurt Weber to share the Vermeer's existence with her. She hadn't been able to get ahold of Vincent, though, so she had called her former boss out of desperation, hoping that he would be able to contact Roelf directly.

"Would you be able to tell the difference between a real Vermeer and a forgery? I read the report you sent to Vincent, and I know Bruno Weber was convicted of selling forged looted art," Huub replied.

"Look, I understand you are skeptical. So was I. But if you saw it, you would know it was by Vermeer. The way he painted the reflections, the transparency of the ruby, it is incredible. I cannot believe it is a fake."

Huub snorted.

"He didn't know I was coming by to ask about it. If he didn't want to give it back, he could have lied or said nothing. Instead, he took me to his private study to show it to me. He's dying and has no one to leave it to after he's gone. I swear, Huub, he almost seemed relieved to return it."

"Seventy-plus years too late."

"That's true. But he said that he has more looted art he wants to return. Let's not make him angry by accusing him of any crimes just yet. Who knows what else he has tucked away! Think about all the families we can help reunite with their artwork. The reason why I'm calling is that he wants proof of Roelf's ownership before he hands the Vermeer over to me. Can you get in touch with Roelf and ask him to send over the rest of his paperwork? Or do you already have it?"

"Roelf sent us everything he has. His proof is the photos Vincent emailed you last week."

"Wait—that's it? Only those three pictures of it hanging in his family's home? Oh, I hoped Roelf had more evidence to back up his claim."

Zelda puffed out her cheeks in frustration. "I wonder if that will be enough to convince Weber. Though he did say he was going to check his ledgers, as well. Hopefully, they will confirm that Roelf's family was the last owner."

"I could call his daughter and ask if they have found more evidence proving their ownership, but I would rather not get her involved unless we have no choice. Roelf's health is worsening, and I know she won't be able to keep this news secret from him."

"If I don't pick up the Vermeer before dinnertime, she will have to deal with the German government. He's turning his entire collection of looted art over to them. I don't have any other choice but to print off the photos and hope Weber accepts them as proof."

"Wait, does Vincent know what you're doing?"

"No, I tried calling him, but he didn't answer. Look, Huub, I know what you are thinking, but I really didn't expect this to happen. I noticed Neue Gallery was close by and decided to see if it was open. Then one thing led to another…" Zelda trailed off sheepishly, certain Huub was mad that she'd taken too much initiative.

"I know exactly how your 'one thing led to another' talk goes. You have always had trouble listening to orders," Huub said, his tone stern.

"I wasn't planning this, but what an incredible coincidence, right?"

"You could say that. Can you at least email Vincent and tell him what you are doing? This is his investigation, after all. Are you certain the handover can't happen tomorrow? I am sure he would want to be there for it."

"I'm sure you're right, but Weber repeatedly said that I had to be back before 6 p.m., or it would be too late. I don't think Vincent can get here from Croatia that fast, and I really don't think Kurt will wait around for him to arrive. He was packing up his bags and said he wanted to spend the rest of his days with his loved ones. I don't think he's coming back to Munich. I bet that's why he was so forthcoming—he's washing his hands of the looted collection. If I don't pick it up tonight, we'll have to submit an official request to the German government or whoever ends up taking responsibility for it. If that happens, I doubt Roelf will get to see it before he passes."

Huub was silent.

"It's your call, Huub. Roelf is your friend, not mine."

"Okay, take Roelf's images to Weber and see what he says. Please call me after you've talked to him. Then we can try to get ahold of Vincent. I would prefer that he have it authenticated before I contact Roelf."

"Excellent. Thanks." Zelda was dancing with joy. Her first real "lost art" assignment and she'd found a Vermeer! What were the odds?

"So, should I call the police and ask for an official escort? I mean, the portrait is worth a lot of money. I won't feel comfortable keeping it in my room until Vincent shows up."

Huub was silent a moment, contemplating her question. "I have a good friend in Munich I can call on. He's an art dealer who helped me with a restitution case years ago."

"Do you trust him?"

"I trust him implicitly. I'll ask him to accompany you to Kurt's and then store the Vermeer in his gallery until I can reach Vincent."

"Honestly, I would feel better if we called the police."

"I would rather not alert the authorities about the Vermeer's existence until we can get ahold of Vincent. I am concerned the police may confiscate it if we do. Or, worse, think that you stole it. Come to think of it, I am going to type up an official release for Weber to sign. If he is as ill as he claims, he may not live long enough for Vincent to arrange the export permit."

"Okay. Listen, I didn't come here for research—I'm actually on vacation with my family," Zelda said, as she caught sight of the souvenir shop. She ran to the window, but didn't see her parents or Jacob inside. Her stomach sank as she peered inside the café and didn't see them there, either.

Oh, no! Did they go back to the hotel or the Hofbräuhaus? she wondered.

They were probably livid with her. But when she told them about her thrilling discovery, she knew they would understand why she had to act so quickly.

"Speaking of which, I need to go. It would be helpful if we can get ahold of Vincent tonight. Would you mind calling his wife to see if she has another telephone number for us to try?"

"I'll give her a call. Let me know what happens, okay?"

"Will do. Talk to you soon." Zelda hung up and allowed herself a happy dance before dialing Jacob's number.

17

Childhood Memories

As soon as Zelda left, Kurt Weber plopped down onto his couch, confused yet giddy. He always believed in fate, karma, serendipity, or whatever people liked to call it these days. Hours earlier, Kurt was ruminating on the owners of his Vermeer when this investigator suddenly showed up and provided him with the details of their past. It felt as if Zelda was a guiding angel sent to let him know he was on the right path. He hoped she was sincere and would return on time with the paperwork he requested. Nothing would give him more joy than to give a painting back to at least one owner before his time on Earth was up.

He glanced at the little black book in his hand. He had read through his father's meticulous notes as a young man, but he had forgotten the details about the Vermeer's provenance. Bruno knew the Konig family well, it seemed.

"1938—property tax debt, Berlin" was the first notation. When the Konigs left Germany for the Netherlands, Bruno had personally cleared out their Berlin home and kept several of their best paintings for himself instead of selling them at auction. The same artworks were now crated up and ready for the German authorities to return to their rightful owners. His father had also been responsible for confiscating the paintings that Konig had loaned to ten German museums, several of which still enriched Bruno's collection.

It seemed that was not the last time their paths crossed. From what Kurt could gather from his father's notes on clearing homes for the Mühlmann Agency, he had asked his boss about the Konigs and mentioned their exquisite art collection.

It wasn't clear from Bruno's notes whether the Konigs had already been rounded up and deported before his father asked about them or whether Bruno's questions were the reason Mühlmann had them arrested. Either way, Bruno was the one who removed the five paintings from the Konigs' Amsterdam home. Though the Vermeer should have been shipped to Linz for the Führermuseum, it found its way into Bruno's collection instead.

Kurt closed the book, filled with a deepening sense of sadness. He imagined much of his father's looted collection came from similar stories.

When Kurt dared ask his father why he had never returned the paintings to their owners, Bruno sat him down and explained how he was afraid others would regard him as a vulture instead of a savior. Seeing his business destroyed, being imprisoned, or even murdered by a relative affected by his actions, was not out of the question.

Now is not the right time, Bruno often said. Kurt wondered whether it would ever have been the right time.

Gunther's death had empowered and emboldened him to make his decision, and Zelda Richardson's visit proved the fates were on his side. They had all profited from their ancestors' plundering for long enough. The entire Network must fall, and the rightful heirs must be reunited with the remnants of their past.

Kurt looked up to a framed photograph of him and his father. For the first time in his life, Kurt was glad Bruno was gone.

Kurt pulled a second suitcase out from under his bed and carried it to his study. He'd already packed up his clothes and placed the case by the door. It was time to clear out his office. He was saving crating up the few real masterpieces still hanging in his home for last.

The contents of his hanging files and desk drawers easily fit into the large leather case. Absently, he flipped on the radio as he pulled the letter to the restitution committee out from under his blotter. Should he mention that the Vermeer had already been returned to Roelf Konig? He tapped his chin, considering, when the radio announcer's voice broke his concentration.

"During a raid by Interpol this morning, artwork stolen from Jewish owners during World War II was found in all three dealers' galleries. Though they deny knowing the artwork was looted, the director of Art Recovery Europe told Channel 5 that it would be virtually impossible for the dealers not to know. All nine paintings are prominently displayed in several lost-art databases."

Kurt's jaw dropped. Because selling looted artwork wasn't technically illegal—more like immoral—he hadn't expected the police to arrest them but to call them in for questioning. That was why he had alerted the media, as well.

So why were they in police custody? Kurt turned on his laptop and searched the news until he found his answer. Unbeknownst to him, the three dealers were already under surveillance because of suspected money laundering and were arrested during a planned raid—not for being in possession of looted artwork.

Kurt roared with laughter. It served them right. His jubilance was tempered by the speed at which the police had acted. He had hoped to be on a plane before the news broke. How long would it take the police or a journalist to figure out that he had brought all nine paintings to the dealers? He could imagine the Swiss men would gladly shift the blame back to him if given the chance. If anyone from the Network discovered what he had done, he might not live long enough to see his plan through to fruition.

His ringing doorbell brought his answer. Kurt slipped the letter back under the leather blotter and walked slowly down the steep staircase.

Kurt tried telling himself that it must be Zelda returning with the documents, but she had been gone less than an hour. Rationality told him to expect another visitor. One look through his peephole confirmed his suspicions.

As silently as he could, he put the suitcase packed with clothes into the coat closet and shut it tight. He did not want his visitor to know he was leaving town.

When the doorbell rang a third time, Kurt answered, his smile bright.

"Hello, Brigitte. What brings you here?"

"Are you serious?" She laughed as she walked past him and trudged up the stairs. "I'm surprised you are still in Munich after that stunt you pulled."

He followed slowly, panting as he climbed. "What do you mean?"

"Don't play dumb." Brigitte turned on him so fast that he almost lost his balance. "The three Swiss dealers."

"I just heard about it on the radio. They said the police have been investigating them for whitewashing."

"And now, thanks to you, they will investigate them for knowingly trading in looted art. Don't you think they may try to strike a deal? Rat out the Network for a lighter sentence?" Brigitte shook her head as if scolding a child. "Why, Kurt? Why did you set them up?"

"I don't know what you're talking about, Brigitte."

"Oh? Is it a coincidence the same three you met with last weekend were picked up by the police for questioning this afternoon? Don't deny it. I've spoken with their assistants, and they confirmed you brought paintings in to sell."

Kurt leaned against the wall and held onto the railing, afraid he might lose his balance out of shock. If Brigitte knew about his involvement, the police must, as well.

She pursed her lips. "I've been told impending death does funny things to your conscience. Some people experience a deep desire to repent for their supposed sins. Is that what this is, Kurt?"

"We shouldn't have kept the artwork for so long, and you know it."

"How could we return it all without destroying all our families' reputations and tarnishing all of their achievements?"

"We're vultures, Brigitte, picking at the bones of the dead. All of us. This has to stop."

"You're being naïve. The heirs are the vultures. The true owners passed away long ago. Our parents and grandparents saved them from Hitler. If they hadn't hidden them away, all of the artwork would have been destroyed, burned, or sold abroad. We are the ones who have made so many sacrifices to keep them safe."

Brigitte stood at the top of the stairs, pacing. It was making Kurt nervous. "You know as well as I do most of these claimants aren't anything more than money-grubbers. Most hadn't even met their relatives or, worse, married into the family. They are the real profiteers, not us or our forefathers. After everything our families have done to protect and care for them, don't we deserve the paintings more than the second-once-removed of some dead man? These claimants are only going to sell the art to the highest bidder and live off the profits."

"How can you say that? At least they have some connection with the real owner. We are the money-grubbers, Brigitte. Why can't you see that? Our forefathers should have turned the art over to the Allies in 1945, not kept it secreted away. That was the moment it all went wrong—when they went from heroes to profiteers."

Brigitte stared at him, then laughed. "If you feel so strongly, why didn't you return your art to its owners after your father passed?"

"I couldn't..."

"You couldn't destroy his reputation, could you? Yet now that your family line is dying out, you have no trouble destroying ours."

"What's done is done. If only more members had listened to Gunther and agreed to restitution, I wouldn't be forced to do this. You can do whatever you want with yours, but the art my father took is going to be returned. Period."

"How dare you—"

Kurt puffed out his chest, resolute in his decision. "Brigitte, there is no point in discussing this further. My mind is made up. If you will excuse me, I have things to take care of."

Brigitte remained on the top step, blocking the entry to his living room. "Kurt, if one of us is arrested, they will find the rest of us. And all of our reputations and businesses will be destroyed. Your entire life, you've lived off the artwork and never took issue with it, until now. You are the worst kind of hypocrite that exists. I cannot allow you to return your father's collection. Max and the rest agree with me. It's too risky."

"Frankly, Brigitte, I don't give a damn. Leave my home. Now."

Brigitte stood stock still.

"You can't do this," she said, but Kurt held up his hands as if to stop her words.

"I can. In fact, this morning, an investigator was here looking for the Vermeer my father kept. The owner's son has been searching for it for decades!"

Brigitte tensed up. "What is his name? What exactly did you say to him?"

Kurt sneered. "Actually, it was a woman. I told her that the son could have it back. He deserves it more than I do."

"You fool! What have you done?" Brigitte raged. "Do you really think if you return this Vermeer, the private investigator will leave it at that? No. She'll keep digging into your father's past and that of everyone he ever worked with. Unsubstantiated rumors have tied our families together for decades. It won't be difficult for investigators to link us. They won't stop until they have us all."

They won't have to dig far, he thought. In his letter, he named all of those involved in the Network. Brigitte was number two.

Kurt threw up his hands in frustration and began to climb past Brigitte. "There is nothing you can say to change my mind—neither you nor anyone else in the Network."

This was precisely why he had entrusted only one soul with the artwork's location—his friend Helmut.

Brigitte moved in close, nodding sadly. "I was afraid you were going to say that."

Brigitte pushed him so suddenly, Kurt had no time to grab onto the handrail. He jerked back instinctively, stumbling over the steps and plunging headfirst down the stairs he had learned to crawl on. As he tumbled to his death, memories from his childhood flickered through his mind. His final thought was of his first kiss with his grade school sweetheart on the bottom step—the same step that snapped his neck.

18

A Few More Days

“Is it true? Did you really find a Vermeer at that gallery?” Debbie asked as she pulled her daughter into her hotel room.

Zelda glanced around the hallway, wishing her mom had been a little more discreet, before closing the door behind them. When she had called Jacob to explain her delay, he had listened patiently and reassured her that he understood, yet made clear that she would have to explain her absence to her parents. Apparently her mother, in particular, was upset that Zelda had deserted them by the souvenir shop. As soon as she had returned to the hotel, she had veered off to her parents' room, instead of first checking in with her partner. Luckily, Jacob had had the foresight to share her good news with her parents before she'd returned.

“It is—or at least, I think it is. Vincent will have to have it authenticated before we can call the heir.”

Debbie fell onto the bed. “That is amazing. So what happens next? I take it Vincent is on his way to Munich.”

Zelda shook her head and sat down next to her mother. “I haven't been able to reach him. But he did say he was chasing down a lead in Croatia. If he is on a stakeout, he might not be able to respond to my messages or voicemails. Which is why I have to go back to the gallery this evening and pick up the painting.”

“What do you mean?” When Zelda hesitated, her mother added, “You said that you handled the paperwork and left the legwork to Vincent. Or did you lie so I wouldn't worry about your safety?"

"No, you're right. Vincent's the detective, not me. Unfortunately, the gallery owner is leaving town tonight and won't wait for Huub or Vincent to fly over. If I don't pick it up tonight, the client will have to submit a claim to the German government. He's quite ill, and I doubt he will live long enough to hear the verdict. I am not blowing you and Dad off; it's really now or never, Mom."

"But a real Vermeer must be worth a lot of money. Shouldn't you call the police or arrange for security? I don't like the idea of you walking around Munich with a multimillion-dollar painting under your arm."

Touched by her concern, Zelda wrapped her arm around her mother's shoulder, hoping her answer would not upset her further. "You are absolutely correct, but Huub doesn't want to inform the police just yet because he is afraid they might confiscate the painting."

When Zelda noticed her mother's face draining of color, she quickly added, "Huub has gotten in touch with an art dealer friend of his who lives in Munich. Unfortunately, he is out of town, but his son, Oskar, is here, and he's a kickboxer. He is going to accompany me."

"That's awfully convenient for Huub. So he's letting you take the risk of getting caught with it? What kind of boss is he?"

"If anything goes wrong and the police get involved, Huub assured me that Oskar will take responsibility for us having the painting. And I'm willing to take that chance," Zelda said. "If it is a genuine Vermeer, this is the opportunity of a lifetime—one I don't want to pass it up."

Truth be told, Zelda wasn't too keen on Huub's plan, either, but he was adamant the police not be involved. She felt as if she had no choice but to trust Oskar. The fact that his father was an important gallery owner and a good friend of Huub's was the only reason why she did.

Debbie bit her lip. "Are you certain you can trust this German kickboxer? Maybe your dad should go with you."

Zelda wanted to chuckle but kept her face neutral out of respect. She loved her dad dearly but doubted a seventy-year-old, out-of-shape realtor would scare off any would-be art thieves. "I appreciate the thought, but I am assuming Jacob will want to go with me, and I'm not sure there will be room for all of us and the Vermeer in Oskar's car."

When her mother's forehead creased, Zelda added, "I can still take you and Dad over to the Hofbräuhaus, but then I'll need to come back here to meet Oskar. As soon as the Vermeer is secure in his father's art gallery, I'll join you for dinner."

"Okay." Debbie pulled her daughter into a hug. "You are right—you can't let this opportunity slip through your fingers. I'll explain everything to your dad once he's done with his shower, but I'm sure he will understand. We'll keep our fingers crossed for you."

Zelda squeezed her mother tight before releasing her and standing up. "Why don't you give me a few minutes to get Jacob up to speed, then we can head over to the Hofbräuhaus together."

Debbie smiled up at her. "That sounds great. See you soon."

19

Confusion on Hackenstrasse

Zelda willed Oskar to drive faster through the busy streets of downtown Munich. It had taken her longer than expected to get her parents settled at the Hofbräuhaus, and 6 p.m. was fast approaching.

Luckily, the waiter placed her parents next to another older American couple, already sitting on one of the long picnic tables situated close to a small podium. A band, wearing lederhosen and green felt hats, was playing oompah music, their enthusiasm infectious. Zelda tapped her foot in time with the melody as she gazed around the enormous structure in awe. She had never seen so many tables indoors before. The many arches were decorated in colorful vines, flowers, and flags. It was somehow cozy despite its massive size.

"Good luck tonight, honey," her dad said when she kissed her parents goodbye.

As she walked away, she heard her mother and the other woman laughing at the tuba player's antics. Everything was going to be okay.

Zelda had then raced back to the hotel to retrieve the folder of printouts and Jacob. His insistence that he accompany her to the gallery had put her and her parents at ease. She was growing increasingly nervous about her upcoming conversation with Kurt, as well as taking possession of a valuable piece of art. Huub may have been a good friend of Oskar's father, but she didn't know either one of them. And unfortunately, she knew all too well what greed could do to a person. It was nice to know that Jacob had her back.

Zelda only hoped that Oskar's car was roomy enough to hold the three of them and the painting. Even though the Vermeer was no bigger than a sheet of paper, Zelda hoped that Kurt Weber had a crate or another sort of protective covering for the painting. The last thing she wanted to do was damage it on the way to Oskar's father's art gallery.

At precisely five thirty, Oskar entered the lobby. She had googled his name earlier and found a headshot, not that it was necessary. He was one of the largest and burliest men she had ever laid eyes on. Luckily, the kickboxer was also quite relaxed and did not seem bothered by Jacob's presence. However, her heart sank when Oskar led them back outside. The beefy man barely fit behind the wheel of his sports car. As she and Jacob squeezed into the tiny automobile, Zelda wondered how they were going to get the painting back to the art gallery. Could they strap a crate onto the roof of the tiny automobile? Or would it be better if she and Jacob followed Oskar to his father's gallery in a cab?

Zelda squeezed Jacob's hand and stared outside, grateful that neither man was feeling chatty. She needed a moment to digest the fact that she was about to pick up a Nazi-looted painting, one created by Johannes Vermeer, no less. The idea was simultaneously electrifying and terrifying.

As glad as she was that Oskar and Jacob were with her, she would have preferred a police escort. Being responsible for what was potentially a multimillion-dollar painting made her incredibly nervous. Whether it later proved to be a genuine Vermeer, she remained convinced that it was the actual painting that they were searching for. How she wished Vincent had responded to her messages—she could have really used his guidance right now. But until he answered her calls, she had to do as Huub asked and not call the police just yet.

Roelf Konig had months to live, not years. No one wanted the Vermeer to get caught up in bureaucratic tape. Huub was convinced Vincent would be able to explain their actions to the proper authorities and, ultimately, arrange for an export permit that would allow it to leave the country—as long as Zelda got Kurt to sign the letter Huub sent over, releasing any claim on the painting.

Vincent was right. Finding the painting was only the first step in a long line of actions that needed to be taken before the Vermeer could be returned to Roelf. She hoped Huub was able to reach Vincent and persuade him to come to Munich as soon as he could. Until he arrived, the Vermeer would remain hidden away in the art dealer's gallery.

Zelda's hands were trembling. She had so many questions for Vincent. Would Huub's letter be enough, or was there something else she should do to prove that Kurt had relinquished any claims on the Vermeer? She certainly didn't want the authorities to accuse her of stealing it from Kurt and trying to smuggle it out of the country.

She thought of calling Vincent again, but it was too late. From the looks of it, they were approaching the Hackenstrasse. Oskar put on his turn signal, then stopped abruptly as a police officer approached his window. Zelda looked around the officer to see that their passage was blocked by red and white tape with the word *Polizei* on it. The officer said something in German to Oskar, who then began backing up.

"What's going on?" Jacob asked.

"This is as far as we can go. The police have blocked off the street in connection with an investigation. I'll park around the corner, and we can walk over together."

Zelda checked her watch. It was already five to six, which meant Kurt was about to walk out of his door. She didn't have time to dillydally if she wanted to recover the Vermeer tonight. She tapped her foot while Oskar parked, and then sprinted back to Kurt's street, where they joined the growing crowd already huddled close to the police tape.

Oskar asked a police officer why the street was blocked off, then translated his response. "A man was found dead in his home. The police are searching the neighboring buildings for any clues to his possible killer, though they are not certain he was murdered."

Zelda took in the number of police officers swarming the street, knocking on doors.

"His body must have just been discovered," Zelda murmured to Jacob.

"That would explain why the crowd is multiplying rapidly," he whispered back. "What do we do now?"

"So we can't go any further?" Zelda asked the policeman in a loud voice.

The young man answered in German, which Oskar quickly translated for them. "No, I'm afraid not."

Zelda swore under her breath as she pulled out her phone. She dialed Kurt's number, but there was no answer. Her nervousness bubbled to the surface. She had come this far; police tape would not deter her recovery efforts. She turned her attention to a slightly older police officer and pleaded, "I urgently need to speak to a man who lives at number 15, apartment 1C, but he is not answering his phone. Is there any way you could let him know that I'm standing outside his door?"

The officer's eyes widened slightly before he answered in English. "Why did you have an appointment with Kurt Weber?"

Zelda was startled to hear that the policeman knew who lived in that apartment. "I am here to pick up a painting on behalf of a client."

"Please wait here, miss," the officer said before taking two steps away. He kept an eye on Zelda as he spoke into his walkie-talkie. Soon, an older man in a gray suit approached the police tape and quietly chatted with the officer. Based on his age and appearance, Zelda figured he was the detective in charge. He came over to Zelda. "Hello, I am Inspector Bauer. This officer tells me you had an appointment with Kurt Weber?"

Zelda hoped both men's use of the past tense was merely a deficiency in their English. "Yes, that is correct."

He held up the tape. "Could you please come with me. I have a few questions for you."

Zelda shook her head. "I'm happy to cooperate, but can you first tell Mr. Weber that I haven't forgotten him? He is leaving town in a few minutes, and it is imperative I speak with him before he does."

Inspector Bauer leaned in close and said in a soft voice, "I would, except we found Mr. Weber dead in his home twenty minutes ago. Would you please follow me?"

Zelda froze in shock. Dead? How could that be? He was obviously sick, but she didn't have the feeling he was so ill that he would die within a few hours. The inspector waved her under the tape, then strode off toward a small tent set up across from the entrance to number 15. She and Jacob began to follow when Zelda realized Oskar was still on the other side of the tape.

"Aren't you going to join us?" she called out.

"I heard what the officer said," Oskar said. "Do you want me to wait for you?"

"I have others to interview," the inspector yelled.

"I guess there's no reason for you to wait. It doesn't look like we will be picking up a Vermeer tonight," Zelda replied to Oskar, saddened by this realization. As terrible as it was to hear about Kurt, she wondered what his demise would mean to Roelf's claim. The police certainly wouldn't be so willing to hand a Vermeer over to anyone based only on a few blurry old photographs.

"We'll take a cab back to the hotel. Thanks, Oskar."

He waved then disappeared into the large crowd as she followed the inspector to the tent. He held the tent flap open for her and Jacob. Inside was a table covered with paperwork, maps, and empty coffee cups.

"We can talk in here. May I see your passports?"

He must have noticed the worried expression on Zelda's face because he added quickly, "I prefer to know who I'm dealing with before we talk about Mr. Weber."

Jacob pulled out his passport as he explained, "I am only here to assist. Zelda had the appointment with Kurt Weber."

The officer studied him and then the photo critically, before handing his passport back and then nodding to Zelda.

She handed over her American passport and Dutch driver's license.

"You're an American living in Amsterdam? Lucky girl. Why did you move there?"

"I came over to study art history and never left. Now I work for Vincent de Graaf. He is a private investigator specializing in art recovery, and this is actually his case. My involvement is accidental."

"Why were you meeting with Mr. Weber?"

Zelda hesitated slightly before deciding to lay all of her cards on the table. "He was in possession of a portrait painted by Johannes Vermeer. It was taken by the Nazis in 1942 from its Jewish owners, the parents of our client. I have his proof of ownership with me. Mr. Weber asked me to bring these documents to him tonight so he could hand the Vermeer over to me."

"I see. May I look at the documents?"

Zelda held her breath as he looked through the sparse paperwork. As he reached the end of the meager contents of her folder, he began to laugh.

"This is it? You expected an art dealer to hand over a multimillion-dollar painting to you based on this?"

Zelda shrugged. "Honestly, I thought the claimant had more proof of ownership before I met with Kurt Weber. I can't guarantee that he would have given me the Vermeer, but he was incredibly amicable to the idea. In fact, when I met with him this afternoon, he seemed almost relieved to give it back to Roelf. He was more concerned that I return on time than the kind of paperwork I had as proof."

"Why was that?"

"He was leaving town to visit relatives. That's why I had to come back before 6 p.m. I assumed it was so he wouldn't miss his flight or train."

"To where?"

"I didn't ask, and he did not say. He only said that he wanted to spend his last days with his loved ones. He was dying. From the looks of it, I would say he had cancer."

"That's interesting. Our officers could find no living relatives. Did you see any packed bags?"

"No, but I was only interested in the Vermeer."

"And were there paintings hanging on all of the walls in his home when you visited this afternoon?"

Zelda thought a moment. "I do recall seeing paintings in his gallery, kitchen, living room, and home office. But I was so focused on the Vermeer that I didn't really notice the rest of his furnishings."

"And was this Vermeer hanging across from his desk?"

Was hanging? Zelda felt a tinge of fear. She'd assumed it would be difficult to gain access to the portrait now that the police were involved, but she'd never considered that it could be missing again. "Yes, it was. Inspector Bauer, is the Vermeer inside the apartment or not? If it has been stolen, my client will want to know."

"I am afraid it's not that simple. Several paintings have been removed from the walls, including the one that was hanging across from his desk. But we don't yet know if they were stolen."

"I don't get it. Either the painting is up in his apartment, or it's not," Zelda said, unable to disguise the irritation in her voice.

The inspector's eyebrows shot up. "As I said, the paintings are no longer hanging on the walls. At first, we assumed that Mr. Weber was the victim of a robbery until we checked the fire going in his hearth. From what we can tell, seven paintings were burned before we arrive."

Zelda's jaw dropped. "Are you saying Kurt Weber burned the Vermeer?"

The inspector shrugged. "We don't know yet. Our forensic team will need time to sift through the remnants, but it is clear that several different frames were still smoldering when we arrived. The canvases would have burned up more quickly."

Zelda was glad she was sitting. Otherwise, she might have fainted. "Oh my God. How could this happen?"

"I cannot yet answer that."

"Then how did he die? A heart attack or stroke?"

"We are not certain. His body was found at the bottom of his staircase. There are no obvious signs of foul play. And in light of your testimony, I am now convinced that he fell down the stairs before he could finish burning all of the artwork in his home."

"Why would he do such a thing?"

The inspector cocked his head. "Mr. Weber's father, Bruno, was arrested for selling a forgery to a well-known politician. It could very well be that the Vermeer was not what you thought it was, but one of his father's fake paintings."

Zelda felt as if she had been sucker-punched in the gut. "Which would mean he was going to give me a fake Vermeer but must have had second thoughts. How could anyone be so cruel?"

"I ask myself that question almost daily." The inspector rose. "Thank you for cooperating, Miss Richardson. I'll walk you two back."

Jacob took her hand and squeezed, but Zelda's thoughts were so dark, she barely noticed his sweet gesture. Instead, she followed the detective in a daze, disgusted by human behavior.

After the officer lifted the police tape and waved them under, Zelda shook his hand and thanked him, keeping a brave face despite feeling deflated by this turn of events. Was the Vermeer she'd seen in Weber's study a fake? It seemed like the genuine article to her, but she was no art expert. Yet Weber had seemed so sincere when she had met with him earlier today. The image the inspector sketched of Kurt's intentions didn't mesh with that of the man she'd spoken with. Why would he go through the charade of wanting to give it back if it was a fake? And what about the rest of his looted collection—was that a lie, too?

"I better call Huub and let him know what's happened," she said to Jacob before pulling out her phone.

"Of course. Take your time. I'll see if I can get us a cab."

Her call went directly to voicemail. "Hi, Huub, Kurt Weber is dead. The police are here, and the lead investigator just interviewed me. He seems to think the Vermeer was a fake. In any case, it may have been destroyed—there were several frames burning in the fireplace when the police arrived. I don't know what to think. Could you call me back when you get a chance?"

She hung up and blew out a lungful of frustration. When she turned away from the police tape to look for Jacob, an older man tapped on her shoulder.

"Excuse me, miss. I saw you speaking with the inspector. Did he say when the street would be reopened?" the elderly stranger asked in near-perfect English. He was wearing a red velvet dinner jacket and corduroy trousers that were clearly not intended to be worn outside, based on how badly the man's legs trembled.

"I am sorry, he did not. Do you live here?"

"Yes, in apartment 1E, two floors above Kurt. I heard you asking about him; I was the one who found his body."

"That's horrible! What happened?"

"I wanted to return a book I'd borrowed from him, but he didn't answer so I decided to let myself in. We exchanged keys long ago. Two aging bachelors have to look out for each other."

Zelda nodded in encouragement.

"I tried to open his front door, but it was blocked. When I looked through the post slit, I saw Kurt's body leaning against it. I thought he'd fallen down those steep stairs, but the police said his apartment had been robbed, and the next thing I know, I'm standing on the street. It's the middle of March. You would think they would hurry up," he grumbled.

Zelda pulled her jacket closer. "It certainly is cold. The inspector just informed me that they no longer think it was a robbery. Hopefully, you can go home soon," she said consolingly.

Poor Roelf Konig. It was a good thing Huub hadn't told him about the Vermeer because hearing that it had been burned would break his heart. And if the painting Kurt Weber had shown her was truly in the fireplace, then they would probably never know whether it was the genuine article.

She blew out a lungful, watching it dance in the cold air when an idea hit her. Kurt did say he was going to check his ledgers to see how his father acquired the Vermeer. If Bruno had taken it from Roelf's family home, then they could assume it had been the genuine painting. Yet if Kurt had been lying, there would be no record of it. Knowing what had happened to it would at least bring closure to Roelf and his family. All she or Vincent would have to do was check Weber's archives for that ledger.

"Say, do you know if Kurt Weber had an assistant or co-owner for his gallery?"

"Not that I know of, but I wasn't really interested in all of that. His friend Helmut would know more about the gallery. He used to help Kurt on the weekends and at those art fairs."

"That sounds like the perfect person to talk to. Do you know where he lives or how I can contact him?"

"Sure, he lives on that street." The man pointed to a small cobblestoned lane on their left. He stuck out his hand. "My name is Dieter. I'll walk you over if you want. I've got nothing better to do."

20

Cruel Deception

After Vincent got back to his small apartment in the heart of Split, he poured a glass of whiskey and sat out on the balcony. It was cold, but he didn't care. Even though he had been tailing his suspect for more than a week, the young gangster had slipped past him and had already been spotted by a trusted associate entering Brazil. Another lead—and case—blown. Vincent downed his drink in one gulp. This was not good for his reputation or his cash flow problem. How could the boy have gotten past him so easily?

He rose to pour himself another glass when he noticed his Amsterdam phone lying on the coffee table, its screen blinking, alerting him that there was a new message. Because Zelda was on vacation, he hadn't bothered carrying it around with him. Six new messages from his employee and Huub were on it. The most recent message simply said, "Check your email, then call me."

Vincent dutifully opened his email and was surprised to see several from Zelda and Huub concerning Roelf's Vermeer.

Zelda's emails informed him of Bruno Weber's work for the Nazi regime and his gallery's checkered history, as well as his arrest for selling a forgery. After his death, his son, Kurt, took over the Munich location.

Vincent trudged through the rest of their updates, wondering what warranted the urgent SMS, until he opened the last email. In it, Huub recounted the conversations that he'd had with Zelda earlier that day about her finding the Vermeer in the Munich gallery and her intention to pick it up this evening.

He dropped his phone onto the couch and shook his head. "Leave it to Zelda..." He would've been surprised—amused, even—had she not disobeyed his orders during his absence. Zelda knew better than to investigate any leads—that was his job. She must have had a good reason, he reckoned, though he wished she had consulted him first.

When he had asked her to look into the recently discovered information concerning Roelf's artwork and the auction house in The Hague, he hadn't expected her to find anything useful. So many records were missing or had been destroyed that it was almost a hopeless case, but he hadn't had the heart to tell Roelf that. Instead, he had delayed Zelda as long as possible, almost hoping Roelf would pass away before she could check the archives. It would only result in more heartache if his assistant did find the Vermeer, and Roelf lost his claim on it.

With Huub in London, busy with work on a new exhibition, it had been easy enough to make excuses for why he hadn't yet made time to chase this lead down. But now that his project was winding down, Huub had more time to worry about the Vermeer. Which was why Vincent had finally agreed to let Zelda search for it.

At least it gave his sole employee something to do while waiting for new clients to call. He sensed a distance growing between her initial interest in the work and the realities of the day-to-day grind. It wasn't for everyone. Perhaps she would be better off working for a museum. Vincent didn't give it too much thought. That was for Zelda to figure out. He wouldn't stand in her way if she wanted to move on.

Vincent's drifting thoughts made him lose focus. According to Huub's last email, Zelda was about to pick up the Vermeer from the Munich gallery. What kind of art dealer would hand over a multimillion-dollar painting to a stranger? It couldn't be the real Vermeer but some sort of cruel deception.

Vincent checked his watch. The last email had been sent two hours ago. Zelda should have acquired the painting by now, yet neither she or Huub had gotten in touch. With a sense of impending dread, he picked up the phone to call Huub.

21

What Network?

Kurt's neighbor Dieter was right. Helmut answered the door immediately.

Dieter touched his shoulder and asked something in German. To Zelda, it sounded as if he was asking whether the man was okay.

"*Nein*," Helmut said softly, shaking his head. It looked as if he had been crying.

Helmut appeared to be as old as Kurt was, yet was much taller than his friend had been. He gazed at Zelda and Jacob suspiciously until Dieter explained why they were knocking on his door so late in the evening.

"The police called earlier. Kurt listed me as his next of kin," Helmut said solemnly in halting English, as if to explain his emotional state.

The older man ushered them inside. Once they were in his living room, he frowned at the two strangers, then said something in German to Dieter.

"His English is weak. I will translate for him. Is that all right with you?"

"Of course. Thank you for seeing us. Dieter tells me you were close to Kurt Weber. I am so sorry to bother you at this time, but I have questions about Mr. Weber's gallery that cannot wait."

Helmut bowed his head and nodded.

"I had an appointment with Mr. Weber tonight. He was going to return a painting to me, one I found during my work for a Dutch private detective. It came into Bruno Weber's possession in 1942, after it had been stolen from its Jewish owners by the occupying Nazi force in the Netherlands."

Helmut looked away when she said "Nazi." Zelda waited until Dieter caught up and nodded, then continued.

"Mr. Weber believed that his gallery's business ledgers would confirm the painting's ownership and promised to check them. Unfortunately, he died before we could meet again. Do you know if Mr. Weber had business partners who would know where he kept his gallery's paperwork?"

Helmut nodded thoughtfully before responding.

Dieter translated his words for her. "Kurt did not have a business partner but did work with several gallery owners regularly. Brigitte Vogel and Max Wolf are the ones who Helmut saw most often. Helmut doesn't know the exact nature of their partnership, but he and Brigitte used to chat often on Saturday. He did not speak to Max much, though he was also a frequent visitor to Kurt's gallery."

Zelda wrote both names down in her notebook, assuming Vincent would want to talk to them. "Why did he not speak to Max Wolf?"

Dieter turned to Helmut, repeating the question in German for clarity.

Helmut pursed his lips and answered.

"He said Max is quite arrogant and acts like his superior despite his young age," Dieter said.

"That's good to know. Were Brigitte and Max bringing artwork to Kurt or buying from him?"

Helmut nodded and responded in German.

"Most of the time, Brigitte and Max brought artwork to Kurt, though they sometimes took paintings out of his gallery. The artwork was always packed up, so Helmut doesn't know which artists or pieces they were trading," Dieter translated.

"Is there anyone else, maybe a family member or another friend, who might have access to his gallery's documents, specifically his older inventory lists and sales ledgers?"

Helmut shook his head. Zelda listened respectfully to his long reply before Dieter translated it.

"No, he had no relatives. Helmut thinks Kurt kept all of his business records in his home office. He'd never looked through the documents but knows

Kurt's study is full of archives and old records that date back to the beginning of his gallery."

"Okay. I'll have to ask the police about it. I hope he didn't burn his paperwork, as well."

Helmut cocked his head and asked in heavily accented English, "Why would Kurt burn anything?"

"The police said several paintings had been removed from his walls, and there were frames still smoldering in his fireplace when they arrived."

Helmut sprang out of his chair and began pacing around the living room, swearing in German.

Zelda looked to Dieter, "Why is he so upset?"

"I'm not certain." He did his best to console Helmut but to no avail. Instead, the older man kept babbling in his native tongue.

"What is he saying?" Zelda asked. The high pitch of her voice caused Jacob to lay a hand on her shoulder, reminding her that he was there for her. She wrapped her hand around his and squeezed.

"Helmut says Kurt should have left the Swiss alone. And that the police had not informed him that paintings had been taken or about the burnt frames."

"Taken? No, the police seemed certain that Kurt had burned the paintings before he fell down his staircase."

Helmut barked at Dieter, who translated for Zelda and Jacob. "Helmut says Kurt would never have destroyed his father's paintings. The network must have taken them, just as Kurt had warned him they would."

"What network?" she asked.

Dieter shrugged. "Honestly, I don't understand any of it."

Helmut ignored her. Instead, he turned to Dieter and spoke rapidly in German, his tone insistent.

"He says we have to leave now so that he can pack. He is afraid the network will find him here."

"Wait—what? This doesn't make any sense." Zelda put her hand on the older man's shoulder. "Helmut, who are you afraid of? Who is this network? Which Swiss did Kurt upset? My boss is a private investigator. He can help you."

Helmut began to laugh. "No one can help me now."

"Sir, if you know who else is part of this network, my boss can…"

Helmut walked to his front door and opened it. A freezing wind rushed inside.

As much as Zelda wanted to shake the truth out of Helmut, she realized Vincent would have to do the rest.

"We should probably go," Dieter said, bowing to Helmut as he exited.

"I am so sorry about your friend. If you have a change of heart, I wrote my phone number on the back of this business card," Zelda said, handing Helmut a card advertising Vincent's firm.

Helmut nodded once in acknowledgment but remained silent. He did not accept the card, so Zelda let it fall onto the hallway's carpet in the hopes he would pick it up after they had left.

As soon as they were outside, Helmut slammed the door shut, turned his lock, and flicked off the outside light. Zelda doubted he would get in touch anytime soon.

The falling snow sparkled in the streetlights like falling stars. When they walked back to Hackenstrasse, the police were removing their tape from the street.

"I can finally go home. And just in time, too, because it looks like a nasty storm is moving in." Dieter held out his hand. "Good luck with your search. I hope you find your client's artwork." He pulled out his wallet and fished around for a slip of paper. "Here, this is Helmut's phone number. Kurt gave it to me in case of emergencies. He seems pretty upset now, but maybe later, you can try talking with him again."

Zelda doubted Helmut would help her further but took the paper anyway. "Thank you so much for your help tonight. I really do appreciate it. Take care." Zelda shook Dieter's hand, then watched as he walked up his staircase.

She turned back to the main street, hoping to find a cab when she glanced at her watch.

"Crap!" Her yelp made Jacob and the remaining police force turn.

"Sorry, I didn't realize it was so late." Zelda blushed then grabbed Jacob's hand before running down the street to find a taxi. As a cabbie drove them to the Hofbräuhaus, Zelda turned on her phone and saw several missed calls from her parents and Huub. There was also one new message from Vincent. All it said was, "I'm on my way."

"Great, now he gets in touch," Zelda groaned, hating to be the bearer of bad news. Had Huub already caught him up or was Vincent still under the assumption that she had recovered a looted painting this evening? She began to type in, "Vermeer gone. Dealer dead," when she realized that it was pointless. There would be time enough to catch him up in person, after he arrived. Tonight, there was nothing more any of them could do. And right now, locating her parents was her top priority. Luckily for her, that was an easy quest. Her mother's long and somewhat tipsy message made clear that they had truly enjoyed their night and were now back at the hotel and would talk to her and Jacob in the morning.

Knowing they were safe and sound sent a wave of relief through Zelda's body.

"This has been one hell of a night. You know what, I could use a drink. What do you say we grab a beer at the Hofbräuhaus before we head back to the hotel?"

Jacob hugged her close. "That sounds like a great idea."

22

Hunting for Art

Brigitte Vogel's hands shook as she sorted through the many documents tossed together in Kurt Weber's suitcase. She still couldn't believe that she had killed him. Not that she had gone to his home with the intention of taking his life. But his words angered her so much, the rage welling up inside had been too much to quell. How dare he decide singlehandedly what their next move would be? Especially when his plan involved exposing all of their families' secrets to the world. Without the correct context, they would all be portrayed as monsters and hounded by the media for the rest of their days.

Brigitte skimmed through every document Kurt had saved for a second time, unable to face the facts. All of this paperwork concerned sales made after 1950. There was nothing here to indicate which paintings Bruno Weber had saved, nor where Kurt had stored them. Where were the ledgers, inventory lists, or even bills of sale? Bruno must have kept a record of them somewhere.

The only clue to their possible location was the three sets of keys in the bottom of Kurt's suitcase. Based on their tags, they appeared to open Kurt's two homes and a storage unit. *Could it be that easy?* she wondered, dreaming of opening the door and finding an art collection to rival that of any major museum.

A knock on her front door brought her to a standing position. Max was right on time. After she'd returned from Kurt's home, she'd called him and explained what had happened. As promised, he was here to help her figure out what to do next. They assumed Kurt had inherited hundreds of looted paintings from Bruno and that he still had most of them in his possession. They just didn't know where he had hidden them away.

"Brigitte, how are you holding up?" Max's kiss was as tender as his words.

Brigitte longed to embrace him but was afraid it would only put him off. She had always had a crush on him, but until recently, he hadn't responded to her advances, no matter how obvious. It was only after Gunther's tirade that he asked her out to dinner.

"I guess I'm okay. I've never caused a man's death before."

"It was an accident, right? From what you said, it sounds like you had little choice. We've all worked too hard to keep this Network's existence a secret."

Brigitte bobbed her head vigorously. "Exactly. He had no right to expose us all." She turned to wipe away a tear, knowing Max did not appreciate displays of emotion.

"You did the right thing. I'm only sorry you were forced into that position." He held her tight, stroking her hair until her calm returned. Brigitte reveled in his touch and the scent of his skin. "Do you really think he was going to give all of his father's artwork to the government?"

"He seemed quite serious." Brigitte thought back to his resolute words and determination. "I have no doubt he was planning on it. But where are they? I haven't found a single mention of Bruno's collection in any of the documents or ledgers that he had saved."

Max nodded to the suitcase full of paperwork. "Are you certain this is everything from his study?"

"No, Kurt had packed this bag before I arrived."

"Was there another suitcase? Perhaps he had already packed up the rest before you arrived."

Brigitte thought back to what she had seen in Kurt's rather small apartment. "I can't recall seeing any other packed bags. But Kurt hit the door hard, so I was worried his neighbors may have heard the fall and would investigate or call the police. As soon as I confirmed he was dead, I grabbed that suitcase and one painting, and left via this gallery. I didn't feel as if I had time to thoroughly search his entire apartment."

Max pursed his lips. He nodded toward the paperwork on her coffee table. "What have you discovered so far?"

Brigitte sank onto her couch. "Not much. He inherited an old farmhouse in Stuttgart and an apartment in Mannheim from his father, and I found a rental contract for a storage unit just outside of Munich. I also found three sets of keys that I assume open all three. There is a chance that the art is in one of those locations, but I haven't found any of his father's ledgers or an inventory list, so we have no way of knowing how much artwork he saved. You would think Kurt would have kept the paperwork at his home, but it doesn't look like he'd packed it in this case."

"I can't believe he would have left those ledgers behind. They may still be hidden in his study—unless the paperwork is with the artwork, wherever that could be," Max said, momentarily lost in thought. He turned to Brigitte and took her hands. "Are you certain he set up the art dealers in Switzerland?"

"I am," she said, her voice strong. "Kurt said he was going to expose us—he used the future tense, not past tense."

"If he was going to expose the Network, why would he act in phases instead of attacking us all at once?"

"Perhaps he didn't think about ratting us out until the media reacted so strongly to the three Swiss dealers. The international attention it garnered might have given him the courage to expose us, as well."

"And what about this private detective?"

Brigitte crossed to her purse and fished out a business card. "I found this card on Kurt's desk. He said a woman stopped by, but this card is for a male detective—Vincent de Graaf. He's Dutch. There is a phone number written on the back. I think the name scrawled above it is Zelda, but it's quite difficult to read."

Max took it out of her hands and examined it. "Indeed. What happened to the importance of penmanship? Do you know what Kurt told this Zelda or Vincent about us?"

Brigitte shook her head. "I don't. Only that a woman investigator stopped by, and that Kurt told her about his father's collection. I only hope she didn't believe him, or that she ends up at the same dead end as us and lets it drop."

Max was silent as he studied her. "Can I see the painting you took from his home?" he finally asked.

He followed Brigitte into the next room. When she flipped on the light in her dining room, it shone down on Vermeer's portrait of a young girl, resting on the table.

Max eyed it skeptically. "Are you certain it is real?"

"Kurt always claimed it was, which is why it was Bruno's prize possession. From what I could see, the rest of the art on his walls and in his gallery is pretty bland and not worth much. His tastes were always quite ordinary."

Max bristled. "You idiot! How could you take a painting hanging inside of his apartment? The police are going to think he was robbed once they notice the empty space on the wall. You said on the phone they thought Kurt lost his balance and fell down the stairs."

"They still do. Kurt was burning old frames when I arrived. He must have forgotten to buy wood again. I took a few of the lesser works from his walls and added them to the fire to throw off the police. There's no reason for them to think it was a robbery. With a little luck, they'll just think he was a crazy old man and leave it at that."

Max relaxed visibly. "Okay, so we're back to square one. Where could Kurt have hidden his father's artwork? I suppose we should check his storage units and homes first."

"That's a great idea. We could make a day out of it." Brigitte's heart began to sing at the thought of spending a full day with Max.

"It would be faster if we split up. Though I do wonder if the paperwork we are searching for is still in his apartment. Finding that may save us long drives to his other homes. The police might not have taken the contents of his study if they thought his fall was accidental."

Max fell silent for a moment before finally stating, "I am going to go back to Kurt's apartment in the morning and see if I can find any more paperwork. It's almost midnight, so it would be too suspicious if I go now. Perhaps he hid the list of art or information about its location in his study or gallery."

"I can go with you."

Max held her hand tight. "No. The neighbors might recognize you and call the police. It's better if I go alone."

Brigitte blew out a breath of frustration. "I don't want to just sit here and do nothing. Why don't I go to one of his homes tomorrow and see if I can find anything there? He may have spread the art across several locations in case there was a break-in or fire."

Max nodded. "That's what I have done with my collection and for the same reasons. Tell you what, if I can't find anything at Kurt's place tomorrow, why don't you drive up to Mannheim?"

"That sounds good. I would be happy to do so," Brigitte replied. She was as eager to find the collection as he was. If it were anything like those they had inherited from their grandparents, it would be worth millions.

"We should try to keep this quiet from the rest of the Network. I don't want anyone to get any ideas…" Max said.

"Of course." Brigitte bobbed her head vigorously. "Though I doubt any of the others will go rogue like Kurt did. Not after what happened to Gunther. The rest understand that we have to stick together." Brigitte leaned in, hoping for a kiss.

Max stood up. "I'm glad you called, Brigitte. I'll ring you as soon as I get back from Kurt's place, and then we can discuss our next move."

Brigitte practically swooned at Max's use of the plural. Instead, she rose and squeezed his hand. "Good luck."

He pecked her cheek. "*Danke schön.*"

23

Vincent Arrives in Munich

"Hi, Zelda. You really landed in the middle of it, didn't you?" Vincent de Graaf smiled as he squeezed her shoulder, his eyes twinkling. Not in delight but because he was on the hunt.

Zelda had just scooped a spoonful of fluffy eggs onto her plate when her boss entered the breakfast room. Her boss grabbed a plate and began loading up.

Late last night, Vincent sent word via SMS that he would arrive in Munich after midnight and had booked a room at the same hotel she was staying at. She had planned on knocking on his door before they left for the day, but running into him at the breakfast bar was even better. He looked exhausted, and his typically neatly pressed clothes were rumpled. Other than that, he was the same old Vincent.

"I'm glad you were able to come over. What happened in Croatia with the suspect you were trailing?" she asked.

"It was a bust." His expression darkened, but before he could elaborate, Zelda's mother pushed her way in between them.

"Hello, I am Debbie Richardson. You must be Vincent. It's good to finally meet you in person!"

"Mrs. Richardson, it is a delight to meet you, as well. I have heard so many wonderful things about you and your husband. And I know Zelda couldn't wait for you to arrive." He took Debbie's hand and kissed it, then gave her his most winning grin.

"Thank you for allowing your daughter to chase up a lead during your vacation."

Debbie's expression tightened. "I'm just glad she didn't get hurt last night."

"It's not Vincent's fault, Mom. He didn't ask me to visit Neue Gallery. I did that of my own volition," Zelda admitted.

Vincent chuckled. "It does get under your skin. There's nothing more exhilarating than chasing a stolen painting, and to find a Vermeer is nothing short of a miracle. I bet you're proud of your daughter."

"Both her dad and I are extremely proud of her, whether she finds a Vermeer or not."

"Hello, Vincent. It's good to meet you." Terry had made his way over to them and was holding out his hand to the private detective.

"You, too, sir." Vincent shook it heartily.

"Say, I don't mean to be rude, but our bus leaves in twenty minutes, and we should eat something before we go. It's a long ride to Neuschwanstein Castle, and I don't see any food stops planned for the ride over."

"Do you need Zelda's help today?" Debbie asked, her voice laced with concern. "I would hate for her to miss this trip, if she didn't have to. Her father and I are only in Europe for a few more days before we have to go back to the States."

Vincent squeezed Zelda's shoulder. "She is all yours. It must have been a real inconvenience, but I appreciate your understanding. Without Zelda's quick thinking, we might not have had any leads to follow."

Zelda glanced at her watch, noting the time. "Say, Mom, give me five minutes to catch Vincent up on all the details and then I'll come join you for a quick bite."

"No problem, dear." Her mother pecked her on the cheek before following Zelda's father back to their table.

Zelda turned to her boss. "Is it going to be a problem if I go to the castle with my family?"

"Definitely not. Based on the information you gathered about Neue Gallery, the dead dealer, and the missing Vermeer, I will need to talk to the German police first, and see what they can tell me about their investigation, his background, gallery, and death before I can do anything. Did anything else happen last night that you haven't already emailed to Huub and me?"

"No, the update about my visit to Helmut and the police interview was the last one."

"I don't understand how Helmut fits into the picture. Who is he?"

"He was Kurt's best friend and helped out with the gallery on the weekends. Kurt's neighbor took me to visit him. I thought he might know who has access to the gallery's paperwork, but Helmut didn't know of anyone, except maybe Brigitte Vogel and Max Wolf. He thinks all of Kurt's business papers were in his study, which probably means the police took whatever they found with them. I hope they will share with you any details they found about his father's secret collection."

"If they found any."

"What do you mean? Don't you believe that Kurt had more looted artwork to return?"

Vincent shrugged. "I don't know what to think right now. Let me talk with the police first and see what they can tell me about Kurt, Brigitte, and Max, before we jump to any conclusions."

"Okay," Zelda replied, a bit flustered by his remark. She had expected him to be as excited as she was by her discovery. She started to rise, but Vincent stopped her.

"Before you rejoin your parents, why did you talk to Helmut instead of emailing his contact information to Huub and me?"

"After the police interviewed me, one of Kurt's neighbors told me about Helmut and offered to take me to his house. What was I supposed to say—no thanks? It all happened so fast, and besides, you were unavailable, remember?"

Vincent glared at her but kept his tone professional. "Your idea to ask about any gallery assistants and Kurt's paperwork was a sound one. I'll see if the police confiscated any of it. I would like to talk to Helmut. Do you have his address?"

"Yes, and his phone number. Do you know if Huub already told Roelf

Konig about the Vermeer?"

"I doubt it. Roelf is far too weak to cope with this news. I would rather we not tell him or his daughter about this discovery until we actually have a genuine Vermeer in our hands. Can you write down Helmut's contact information for me?" Vincent pulled a small moleskin notebook out of his jacket pocket and handed it to her.

Zelda chuckled at how old-fashioned he was as she scribbled Helmut's phone number and address into the little black book. "If you don't speak German, bring a translator. He didn't speak much English. I don't know if he is still in town. As soon as he heard about the paintings being burned, he told us to leave so he could pack his bags."

"As soon as you told him, you mean."

"Yes, well..." Zelda looked away, embarrassed.

"Do you know where Helmut was planning on going?"

"No, he didn't say." She hung her head. "You would have waited and tailed him, wouldn't you? I was so focused on checking in with my parents, I didn't even think to stick around and follow Helmut."

"Don't beat yourself up about it. You did what you had to do. What about the two people he mentioned—Brigitte Vogel and Max Wolf? What can you tell me about them?"

"Only their names. Helmut said they often had artwork with them, so I imagine they are dealers or gallery owners. But I didn't ask him specifics."

Zelda felt so embarrassed. Reviewing the conversations like this made her realize how many things she should have asked Kurt and Helmut when she had the chance—questions Vincent would not have forgotten. Helmut had probably left town by now, which only created extra work for her boss.

"Great, I'll ask the police about them, as well." Zelda looked up to see Debbie waving at them.

She rose and gave her mother a thumbs-up. "I better have some breakfast, otherwise my mom is going to be worrying about my appetite all morning." She turned back to her boss, her eyes pleading. "Would you send me a message later and let me know how it goes? I know this is your investigation now, but I would love to stay in the loop."

"Of course. You've brought us this far. Enjoy this trip to Neuschwanstein. I'll text you later."

24

The Art Looting Network

Vincent de Graaf could tell he was going to like the lead investigator, Simon Bauer. He was a typical German—candid and to the point. So far, they had discussed all of the details surrounding Kurt Weber's death. From the medical dossiers they had acquired, it was clear that Weber was quite ill. As far as the inspector was concerned, he was an older man who lost his balance, fell down his staircase, and broke his neck. Case closed.

"Then why didn't you find any of his gallery archives in his study? According to Kurt's friend Helmut, there should have been decades of business ledgers stored in there."

Bauer smiled. "And when was Helmut last at Kurt's home? Perhaps Weber had them moved to his storage unit since his friend visited. Two of my officers are on their way to the unit now."

"And the missing paintings? Have they all been accounted for?" Vincent asked.

Bauer checked his files, then nodded. "Our forensics team is fairly certain seven different frames were burnt in that fireplace. And seven paintings are missing from his walls. It adds up."

Vincent mulled over the information and nodded in satisfaction. "I can see why you believe Weber burned the paintings before he fell. What I don't understand is what his long game was. Why did he tell my assistant he wanted to return a Vermeer to a Nazi victim if it wasn't genuine? Had he ever been suspected of a hate crime? Is he known as a neo-Nazi or for holding extreme beliefs?"

A smile played on the investigator's lips. "You mean Zelda Richardson? I spoke to her the night of Kurt's death. She's a spunky one."

Vincent laughed. "You can say that again."

"I saw her proof of ownership. If the Vermeer were genuine, then no dealer in his right mind would have given it to her based on that flimsy evidence."

"Yes, well, it sounds like Kurt Weber was not of sound mind or body."

The inspector nodded. "More than you know. My Swiss colleagues informed me that the three Swiss gallery owners all claim that he brought them the looted artwork found in their galleries during the Interpol raid last week."

Vincent snapped his fingers. "Do you mean the three Swiss dealers arrested for money laundering? I saw something on the news about it. I didn't realize Kurt was involved."

"Yes, that's what I mean. Kurt had sent a rambling letter to the local police and media implicating the Swiss in an underground network of art dealers, curators, and museum directors that have been trading in confiscated looted art since World War II. But Interpol had already planned a raid before Kurt sent us that letter. The Swiss authorities are now looking into the art dealers' histories and activities, but them having the looted artwork is more of a moral question than a legal one. I doubt they will serve any time for that crime, though I do expect that the nine paintings found in their galleries will eventually be returned to their owners."

"Ah, yes, the secret art looting network of old Nazis." Vincent chuckled, curious to see how the inspector would react. "I have to say, I am not one of those who believe it exists. But hey, you are on ground zero. Do you believe there are any truths to those rumors?"

As expected, Bauer grinned and shook his head. "No. We run down every new lead that comes our way just to keep the conspiracy theorists off our backs. But we have yet to find any substantial evidence backing any of them up."

"I thought as much. It sounds like Weber was planning on playing a vicious trick on my assistant and client. I wonder why he changed his mind and burned the supposed Vermeer instead."

"Perhaps he grew a conscience."

"Could be. I read that Kurt's father, Bruno, was arrested for selling a forged painting, and to a politician, no less."

"Indeed, we are waiting to hear if the nine paintings found in the Swiss dealers' galleries are genuine or copies," Bauer answered, as if he had read Vincent's mind. "Based on the information I could find here at the bureau, Bruno never revealed who forged the artwork. After he served his jail sentence, he returned to his home and was killed soon after in a motorcycle accident."

"And that's when his son, Kurt, reopened the gallery?"

"Yes, that's what I understand."

Vincent threw one leg over his knee and leaned back. "What can you tell me about Brigitte Vogel or Max Wolf?"

The inspector seemed to freeze momentarily. "Why are you asking?"

"Kurt told my assistant that he wanted to turn over a larger collection of WWII looted artwork to the German government. After his death, a neighbor of his told her that Wolf and Vogel were frequent visitors. I hoped to ask them about his claims."

"Wait, are you saying that Weber also claimed to have a large collection of looted artwork and wanted to turn it over to the authorities?" The inspector sank back into his chair, the shock on his face unmistakable.

"Yes, that is what he told my assistant. Have you found any indication that he was in possession of more art?"

"None whatsoever. Though Weber did own two homes outside of Munich. I will send men to both locations, in case he did have artwork stashed away. But how do Brigitte Vogel or Max Wolf fit into your investigation?" the officer pressed.

"I'm not certain that they are part of this. All I know is that Kurt's neighbor claimed they worked with Kurt often. Based on your reaction, you've heard the names before. What can you tell me about them?"

Bauer leaned back in his chair and folded his hands into a steeple. "Well, both are successful art dealers and respected citizens. They are active on the boards of several volunteer organizations and give generously to charities."

Vincent cocked his head. "Huh, you didn't even need to look them up. So their good deeds are well known?" He always got a bit edgy when dealing with this sort of suspect. If Max and Brigitte contributed heavily to much-loved local organizations, they might be able to intrude upon, or even steer, his investigation.

Bauer rocked back and forth in his chair. "Yes, they are a couple to contend with."

"Oh, are they married?"

"I don't think they are married, but they do attend many charity events together. I believe they are dating, but I'm not a socialite or columnist. Trust me, Vincent, their donations don't give them a free ticket. No one is above the law. Though I do sometimes think they are doing their best to prove they are good German citizens as a way of atoning for their grandparents' sins."

"What do you mean?"

"Wolf's grandfather and Vogel's grandmother were both art advisors to Adolf Hitler. They owned successful galleries in Munich in the 1930s and sold the kind of paintings Hitler preferred, which was how they met. Thanks to their connections to Hermann Göring and Eva Braun, they both became extremely wealthy. After the war ended, their galleries continued to thrive despite their Nazi ties. It did help that they had gone through the denazification process and had even worked at the Allies' Central Collection Point, helping to return confiscated art to its owners. The same can be said of many other galleries in Munich that are still open today."

Alarm bells began ringing in Vincent's head. If they worked at the Allies' CCP, they had free access to all of the artwork that had been confiscated from across Europe. There were several known instances of corrupt dealers stealing art from the CCP, instead of returning it to their owners. He would definitely need to chat with both Brigitte and Max about their grandparents.

The police inspector locked eyes with Vincent. "What are you planning on asking Max Wolf and Brigitte Vogel?"

"I am curious to know if Weber ever mentioned the larger collection to them, and if they might know where he could have kept his father's gallery ledgers. It sounds like they were Kurt's most frequent visitors."

The inspector bit his lip. "Yes, well, we are also searching for the paperwork—you'd do better to ask us about it, than them."

Vincent cocked his head at the inspector, unhappy with the officer's response. "You are asking me not to speak to them?"

Bauer coughed and leaned forward. "Of course not. However, I do want to remind you that Vogel and Wolf are upstanding citizens who are unfortunately burdened with a horrible past. This third generation is doing all it can to put distance between them and their forefathers. And I applaud and respect their actions. I do ask you not to pester them about their grandparents. Keep your questions focused on Weber."

Vincent's forehead creased. Come to think of it, he wasn't so keen on this inspector after all. "It's Weber I'm interested in, not them. It appears they visited Kurt's gallery on a regular basis and I hope they can help me get a handle on what kind of man he was. I am not interested in dredging up the past unless it is required. And in this case, I don't see what their grandparents' histories have to do with the current case," Vincent fibbed, reasonably certain that their past—as well as Weber's—was crucial to this case.

"Excellent." The inspector's expression lightened as a smile spread across his face. He stood and offered Vincent a hand. "I wish you much success with your investigation. When we find Weber's paperwork, I'll get in touch."

25

Monuments Men at Neuschwanstein

"Where's the castle?" Zelda's dad squinted as he craned his neck upward.

"At the top of the mountain, sir," their bus driver responded patiently.

Zelda couldn't fault her dad for asking because the thick forest of evergreens shrouded in mist was impossible to see through. As the driver walked them to the head of the switchback trail that led straight up the mountain, Zelda wondered whether they had golf carts available.

They trudged up the path, winding through the snow-covered trees. A thick blanket of white covered the ground. Occasional showers of snow rained down from the highest branches, its weight finally too much for even the thick limbs to hold.

A cold wind whipped through their winter jackets, but thankfully, there was no precipitation. Their path seesawed over the hills, giving them glorious glimpses over the Alps as they crested one, before the trail plunged them back into the forest.

"It's so beautiful," her mother said, her tone hushed.

Zelda nodded in agreement. They had left the hotel at 8 a.m., so it was still early and cold enough that Zelda could see her breath. She wrapped her arm through Jacob's and snuggled close. He grinned at her and kissed her forehead. The moisture from his lips crystalized into ice almost instantly.

At her parents' insistence, she'd set her phone to vibrate. It took all of her willpower not to pull her phone out to check for new messages from

Vincent, who was currently at the police station meeting with Inspector Bauer. Zelda couldn't wait to hear what the officer had to say about Weber and his missing artwork. She refused to believe Kurt had lied to her or that he had thrown a genuine Vermeer into the fireplace. Who could willingly destroy such beauty?

"What the heck is that?" her mother exclaimed when they rounded a bend near the top.

Zelda's eyes followed her mother's outstretched arm. Through the thinning tree line, they could see almost all of the gigantic castle. However, her mother was not pointing at Neuschwanstein but a glass bridge stretching over the wide valley the castle was built next to.

Zelda's stomach plummeted at the sight. "That's terrifying," she called out, hating the crippling effect her fear of heights had on her.

Her mother ignored her and walked nonchalantly out onto the transparent surface as she pulled out her camera.

"You daredevil," Zelda said teasingly. She let go of Jacob's arm and rushed over to her father. Together, they walked to where the bridge met the mountain. A small sign announced that this was the Marienbrucke. One look through the glass and down into the deep valley below made Zelda's stomach lurch.

"Not for me," she said, taking one large step backward.

Her dad shrugged. "You only live once," he said and trotted out after her mother.

Zelda waited for them on the solid earth, watching as they gestured happily at the surrounding sights. It was great to see they were enjoying their first trip to Europe.

When Jacob caught up, he laced his arm through hers. "I take it you aren't going to join them?"

His teasing tone made clear that he knew full well she would not.

"No thanks, but you go right ahead." She laughed.

"I'm good right here," he said and snuggled closer. "Would you rather be with Vincent right now?"

The uncertainty in his voice made her nuzzle her cheek up against his.

"No way. Being here with you and my parents is far more special than being Vincent's sidekick for the afternoon. Besides, he will fill me in on what he learned later today. And let's be realistic—now that the Vermeer has been stolen or destroyed, there's not much left for me to do. Vincent is the detective; he's going to have to track it down again—not me. I don't want to waste my time following up leads when my parents are only here for a few more days."

"Speaking of which." Jacob's face paled as he looked at his watch. "Why don't we see if your parents want to join the next tour? Our bus leaves in two hours and I would rather not have to rush through the castle."

"That's a good point," Zelda said as she steered them towards the bridge, taking care to stop well before she reached the ravine's edge. "Mom and Dad, shall we visit the castle now?"

"Do we have to?" her dad called back.

"We are ready to go inside. We can meet you after if you prefer," Zelda yelled in response.

"No, we want to stick together," her mother called out before she and her father walked back.

"Oh, Zelda. I know you don't like heights, but wow! What a view. You can see the entire castle from there!" her dad exclaimed.

"I know, but there is supposed to be a great view of the castle just around this next bend," Zelda said.

The travel brochures were correct: the view of Neuschwanstein was magnificent. From this vantage point, the castle was only a few hundred feet away and completely visible. Zelda's breath caught in her throat—to compare it to something in a fairy tale didn't do it justice. She now understood why Walt Disney had used it as a model for his theme park's castle. A multitude of turrets, imposing stone walls, and ramparts were built into the side and top of the sheer cliff face. Zelda had seen plenty of castles since moving to Europe, but none had prepared her for this one.

Her parents' irritation at leaving the glass bridge disappeared quickly. "Will you look at that," her dad said. "It's incredible! How the heck did they build it into the cliff like that?"

Despite the cold weather, groups of visitors continually streamed past them. They joined the flow of traffic, heading to the entrance. The path led them to the front of the L-shaped castle. From the inner courtyards, it seemed as if you could touch the surrounding mountain peaks. It was magical just being there.

The exterior walls and terrace floor were decorated with gorgeous patterns created in tile, stone, and marble. Zelda, her parents, and Jacob joined a long line snaking through the lower square toward a security check. As they approached the front, Zelda saw how groups were being created for guides to lead into the castle. After a short wait, it was their turn.

The interior was nothing short of a sensory overload. Every room was lavishly decorated in vastly diverse styles and themes. Each was so well executed yet different from the next that merely walking from one room to the other was jarring. Their guide informed them about the castle's long history as they moved through the rooms at a clipped pace, including how it was used to house looted art during WWII. As he led them through the Throne Room, the guide explained that the owner was rumored to have been a Nazi sympathizer and good friends with Hermann Göring.

When they walked past the grand staircase, Zelda had to stop and stare.

"What is it?" Jacob whispered into his ear.

"Several famous photographs of the Monuments Men holding looted masterpieces were taken on that staircase. They stood right there. It's so strange to see it in real life." Zelda gazed at the grand staircase, wondering whether Roelf's Vermeer had ever passed through these halls.

"Really? That's crazy! You'll have to show me some of the photos later."

"Oh, Zelda, this is all too much to take in!" her mother gushed as she wrapped an arm around her daughter's waist. "This castle, the decorations, and all this history. It's even more gorgeous than I imagined it would be."

"Great idea to come here, pumpkin. It really is exceptional," her dad added.

"I'm so glad you are enjoying it." Before she could ask what they liked the most, her phone began to vibrate in her back pocket. She snatched it out of her back pocket and checked the screen. "It's Vincent. I should take this."

"No problem. I'll keep an eye on your parents. Catch up with us when you're done."

That boy is a keeper, she thought as she gave her boyfriend a peck on the cheek and then stepped away to take the call.

"Hey, Vincent. What did the German police have to say?"

"Kurt Weber fell down the stairs after he set fire to several of his father's forgeries. Case closed."

"You can't be serious! The police aren't even going to consider that he was pushed?"

"There's no evidence to prove otherwise, Zelda. I've talked with the lead investigator and reviewed everything they had. There is no evidence that another person was present when the paintings were set on fire, nor that Kurt was pushed down the stairs. Given his age and poor health, it is very plausible that he stumbled and fell down. It's going to take their lab quite some time to test the remains of the paintings in his fireplace, but the number of frames does match the number of paintings taken off his walls."

"Kurt wasn't lying to me! He genuinely wanted to return the Vermeer to Roelf. If only I could have convinced him to hand it over to me when we first met."

"Zelda, don't you get it? The Vermeer he showed you must not have been genuine, but one of Bruno Weber's copies. You know as well as I do that Kurt's father was arrested for selling a forgery of a painting missing since WWII. That's pretty sick in and of itself. Who knows how many more fakes he had in his possession? The fact that Kurt asked you to return at six is revealing. He must have been planning on leaving before then, figuring you would return to an empty apartment with the fake painting smoldering in the fireplace."

"Vincent, I wish you could have spoken to him. Then you would understand why I don't believe you. What did the inspector say about the Network?" she said, resolute in her stance.

"Your own research shows that Bruno Weber was convicted of selling forged art. As much as I want to believe your version of events, I cannot fathom that an art dealer would hand a priceless masterpiece over to a stranger, especially when that person had no decisive proof that the painting's ownership."

"But Roelf's photographs—"

"What of them? For all we know, his dad could have sold the Vermeer the day after those photos were taken—any decent lawyer could convince a judge of that. Roelf has no real proof of his ownership, Zelda. Which is exactly why I hoped we would never land in this position. Unless we miraculously find a document showing Roelf's father was the last and legal owner, he won't ever set eyes on that Vermeer."

When Zelda opened her mouth to retort, her boss spoke over her. "Regardless of the ownership conundrum, I cannot believe Kurt Weber was going to hand over the Vermeer to you based on the photos Roelf sent over. It's worth millions, and you are a complete stranger. Why should he have believed you? Unless the painting was a forgery and it was a vicious joke he was planning on playing."

"That might explain why he burned the painting—if he did, that is," Zelda said, keeping her voice neutral. It was clear Vincent didn't believe her, but she was still convinced Helmut and Kurt were telling her the truth. "But why did Helmut react as if he were terrified of this network?"

"What network? Helmut didn't explain to you what he meant, correct?"

"No, he didn't. However, I searched online last night and found out something interesting. After German authorities discovered Cornelius Gurlitt's collection of stolen art in his Munich apartment, there were several articles about a network of Nazi art dealers who stole art earmarked for Hitler's Führermuseum, which they later sold for a profit. Max Wolf and Brigitte Vogel's grandparents were supposedly part of this same network of old-Nazi dealers, along with Gurlitt and Bruno Weber."

"Right, the underground network of Nazi dealers," Vincent said, chuckling.

"Why are you laughing?" Zelda demanded.

"It's the holy grail in the art recovery world. Since the war, there have been persistent rumors circulating about an art looting network based in Munich, consisting of art dealers and experts who worked for the Nazis. Conspiracy theorists claim this group was responsible for stealing thousands of masterpieces from Nazi storage spaces and keeping them hidden from the

Allies after the war. Some believe this underground organization continues to operate today. After Gurlitt's collection was discovered, and it became known that it included many pieces thought to have been destroyed during World War II, these rumors intensified. The discovery has revived worldwide interest in these missing pieces, but there is no proof the network still exists or ever did. Yet some detectives spend all of their free time searching for clues about it. So far, no one has unmasked them. With all of those professionals looking, I have trouble believing there are still thousands of looted paintings hidden away."

"That's what everyone said when they discovered Gurlitt's collection."

"True, but I seriously doubt there are more of those massive collections secreted away. There would be more clues, rumors, and chatter about them."

"I also found articles stating that everyone in Munich knew about Gurlitt's secret collection, and Helmut is convinced that this network exists. And Kurt said he had hundreds of looted paintings he wanted to return, so that's another one in a million chance for you." Zelda couldn't keep the sarcasm out of her voice.

"And where is this collection? Not in his apartment, apparently. And what was he burning in his fireplace? It doesn't sound like hundreds of frames were smoldering in the embers."

"You're right," Zelda conceded. "The art in the fireplace is weird. But I believe he was telling the truth about his collection and wanting to give the Vermeer back. He was so sincere, Vincent. And he was dying. Why would he lie about the Vermeer being genuine or having all that art hidden away?"

"We've talked about this before. You have got to toughen up. You are too easy to take advantage of. People lie all the time and for the stupidest reasons. You have to listen more critically and be more skeptical."

"Kurt was not crazy or unstable. He was doing the right thing because he knew he was dying. He was not trying to pass a forgery off on me. If the cops think he was anything but genuine, then they must be in on it."

Vincent chuckled. "Okay, Zelda. You're getting delusional. Or perhaps you're a little too close to this one. There is no network or secret collection, and the Vermeer was a forgery. Let it go and enjoy your family vacation."

"Why are you giving up so easily? However Kurt died, it doesn't mean he was lying about having a large collection of looted artwork. He said he was going to turn it over to the German authorities. Yet he didn't have hundreds of pieces of art in his apartment. Maybe they are being stored at one of his other homes. Helmut confirmed that the network and collection exist. We have to talk to him before we give up."

"Zelda, no one is giving up. But I have to make you understand that there is no evidence to support Kurt's or Helmut's claims. The police did discover that Kurt owned two homes and rented a storage unit outside of Munich. They are going to visit all three in case he had secreted away a vast collection of looted art at one of them. But neither the police nor I are holding our breath on this one. If he possessed any real masterpieces, why was he living in a run-down apartment full of threadbare furniture? Besides, if such a network existed for three generations, there would be leaks. It's inevitable within any organization."

"I can tell by your tone that you don't expect the police to find anything."

"No, I don't. Because, as an experienced investigator and in light of all the evidence, I agree with the police that there is no evidence pointing to foul play. And nothing they have found indicates that Kurt was anything but a second-rate art dealer with a Nazi sympathizer for a father. Period."

"If the artwork isn't in one of his homes, Brigitte or Max may know where it is," Zelda said, doggedly.

"Which is why I am on my way to Max's gallery. Brigitte is next."

Zelda sighed in relief. "Thank you. I'll call Helmut again."

"If he gets back to you, let me know. But, Zelda, if he doesn't have the art or doesn't know where it's at, we're at a dead end. After you call him, try to forget about this."

Vincent hung up before she could respond. She smiled and shook her head, glad he wasn't going to give up altogether. Zelda quickly dialed Helmut's number, but it went straight to voicemail. She swore under her breath as the familiar message played, then left another plea for him to get back to her as soon as he had the chance.

When she hung up and looked around, another group of tourists was in the room. Her parents and Jacob were nowhere to be seen. She rushed through the last halls, barely noticing the extravagant decorations and furnishings as she searched the crowds for familiar faces. After she exited onto the outside terrace and spotted Jacob and her parents leaning against the balustrade, soaking up the sun and the views, she breathed a sigh of relief.

"Wasn't that incredible?" her mother enthused when she noticed Zelda approaching. "Our guide really rushed us through the last two rooms. We didn't notice that we had lost you until we were back outside."

Zelda hugged her mom. "No, it's my fault. Vincent called. The police believe Kurt fell down the stairs and that he lied about having a Vermeer. That's it. Case closed."

"Ah, honey, I'm sorry it ended up like this. But I do have to say, it was hard to believe that someone would hand a multimillion-dollar painting over to a stranger."

Zelda hung her head low, embarrassed that she had believed so fully that it was the genuine article. The German police, Vincent, and her parents clearly did not think it was a real Vermeer. So why couldn't she let go of the notion that it was the genuine article?

26

Naughty Boy

"What are you doing, young man?"

Max turned and smiled at the speaker as he opened Neue Gallery's door with a key borrowed from Brigitte. The older, well-dressed man was exiting the apartment above the gallery's entrance, looking down on Max from the stairs above. He had hoped to sneak in without being seen but knew it was better to be friendly and open now that he had been noticed.

"Hello there. Terrible news about Kurt, isn't it?"

The neighbor's mistrust softened to sadness. "Yes, it was a horrible shock. But then, the stairs are steep, and he was quite ill. I can imagine he missed a step and lost his balance. Still, it reminds us all that we're getting older. Well, I am anyway," the man added, as he apparently realized his audience couldn't be more than thirty years old.

"Are you a relative?" the man asked, peering at Max over his half-rim glasses.

"No, we worked together on occasion. He was a good friend of my father. After Dad died, I took over his gallery, and Kurt helped show me the ropes. Bless him." It was partially true. Kurt did try to "explain" how the Network worked, though not nearly as well as his own father had before he passed on.

"Do you know when the funeral services will be held? I would like to go to show my respect. Kurt was always kind to me."

"Oh, uh, I don't know. Sorry." Max felt stupid for not having a better response ready. He wished the man would shuffle on down the street and leave him be.

The older man started to turn, then added as an afterthought, "What are you doing in Kurt's gallery?"

"I promised his niece that I would get the gallery's paperwork in order."

"I didn't know he had any relatives close by."

"She's in America," Max lied.

The neighbor nodded, then trudged slowly down the staircase and street toward the main boulevard.

Max entered quickly through the gallery and pulled the door shut. He stumbled around until he found the light switch. What he saw made his head shake in disgust. He hadn't visited Kurt's gallery for months and was disappointed to see how worthless his current stock was. He always found Kurt's tastes to be quite ordinary, but he usually had a decent selection of canvases worth fifty thousand or more. These were all less than five thousand. He ran his hand across a frame's edge and got a finger full of dust. And not well cared for, either. *Kurt wasn't really running a gallery anymore,* Max thought. *This is more of a setup to make it appear that he was still in business.*

Damn it! Max fumed. If only he had stopped by more recently, he would have seen for himself that Kurt was up to something. Was he even ill? Brigitte insisted Kurt had been diagnosed with a rare form of cancer, but what if that was a lie created to give him an excuse to disappear?

Max looked through the drawers and cabinets in the gallery's small office before deciding there was nothing significant enough to take with him. Everything concerned his current stock, not Bruno Weber's paintings.

The back entrance to Kurt's apartment was luckily unlocked. Max climbed softly upstairs toward Kurt's living room. When he reached the top, he glanced at the few paintings still hanging on the walls, his nose crinkling as he took in their lackluster quality.

Max soon found Kurt's office. There was almost nothing left save a few scraps of worthless papers and old catalogs. Most importantly, there were no business ledgers or titles transfers in any of the drawers or archival cabinets. Had the police cleared it all out, or had Brigitte taken everything Kurt had stored here?

Max sat behind Kurt's desk and leaned far back in the plush leather chair, pondering where the old dealer could have hidden such an extensive collection. Chances were high that the artwork was in one of his other homes. This afternoon, he could head over to Stuttgart and see what Kurt had left behind. He rocked a little as he contemplated his next move, when suddenly the chair gave way, sending him flying backward. Instinctively, he grabbed the desktop, shifting the papers still on Kurt's desk. When the chair righted itself, the blotter had moved, and a slip of paper was sticking out.

Curious, Max lifted the blotter and carefully removed the single sheet of paper. Both sides were covered with Kurt's neat handwriting. "What do we have here?" he asked aloud.

As he skimmed the first paragraph, his eyes shot open. "Oh, Kurt, you naughty boy."

Before coming here, Max had wondered how much of what Brigitte had told him about Kurt's intentions and actions were true. Part of him wondered whether she hadn't killed Kurt intentionally in the hopes of stealing his secret collection and made up a story about him wanting to expose the Network when she couldn't find it.

This letter made it clear that she wasn't lying. In fact, she'd minimized the truth. Kurt wasn't considering exposing the Network—he was about to send a tell-all to the German police and international media that would have laid bare their entire operation and everyone involved.

If this was true, then what Brigitte said about Kurt's involvement with the Swiss dealers must also be true. But why would he set them up first and not try to take down the entire Network all at once—if that was his ultimate plan? Max wondered whether he could have talked Kurt out of taking rash action and possibly have manipulated the location of his father's collection out of him. Max doubted it. Kurt was one of the old guards, bound to protect the art out of a sense of parental loyalty.

Max sat a moment and considered what would have happened if Kurt had sent out this press release. All thirteen dealers named—including himself—would have been questioned by the police and their galleries searched. Their family names and histories would have been dragged through the mud, and those wretched rumors of their involvement in Nazi looting would have once again dominated the headlines. Even if the police didn't find any reason to prosecute them, they would have been pulled through the wringer. Max doubted any of their galleries would have survived such a scandal.

Max flipped the page over and continued reading. His eyes lit up when he saw the address listed in the last paragraph. It wasn't either of Kurt's homes or storage unit but an address in Heidelberg. Not only the artwork, but all of the associated paperwork was stored there.

Jackpot, thought Max, contemplating what he would find hidden away. Based on what his father had told him about Bruno Weber and his exquisite taste in art, he had to assume it would be worth millions.

Max scanned the letter once more for clues as to who else may know about the artwork's location, but there were none.

Kurt's pathetic plea at the end made him laugh aloud. "The dealers involved are guilty of nothing more than harboring the secrets of their fathers or grandfathers. I hope you will be kind to them." Max laughed bitterly. The media was never kind to those trading in looted artwork.

Max reread the address Kurt listed at the end. Should he tell Brigitte what he'd discovered? Max considered it but ultimately decided to take a look first. He checked the address on the map. It was more than four hours away, to the north. Funnily enough, Heidelberg was quite close to Mannheim, the town Kurt had an apartment in. Max frowned as he checked his agenda and noted several important appointments scheduled for this afternoon he would rather not reschedule.

There was no getting around it—he would have to drive up in the morning. A smile crossed his face. Not that it mattered how quickly he acted. Kurt was dead, so the art wasn't going anywhere.

27

Ties That Bind

"Max Wolf?" Vincent de Graaf asked. He stood outside Wolf's gallery, located in the heart of Munich. The sign said "closed," yet all of the lights were on.

The young man opened the door a bit further, curiosity gradually replacing the irritation etched on his face.

"Yes, that's me. What can I do for you?"

"Hi, I'm Vincent de Graaf, a private investigator from the Netherlands," he answered in perfect German. "I was working with Kurt Weber on a case. As you may know, he died two days ago."

"Oh, yes, I did hear about that. Please, come inside. It's freezing." Max stepped back and opened the door.

Vincent entered gratefully. The gallery was stylish and sophisticated, and the building was old and well cared for. *He must have a lot of money if he can afford the rent and interior design,* Vincent thought. One look at the art on his gallery walls made clear where the money came from. It was a superb selection of twentieth-century masters that any museum would love to own.

As the front door opened, a large man dressed in black rounded the corner, looking Vincent up and down. He glanced at Max, who nodded and waved him out of the room.

"My assistant," Max explained, turning to Vincent. "It was a shock to hear about Kurt's accident. But then, he was quite ill. Would you like a cappuccino?"

"Thank you."

Max made two coffees that would have made any barista proud, using an old espresso machine located close to the back of the gallery. He poured the milk with the flick of a wrist, creating a leaf in the foam, before setting it down on a triangular table.

Max ushered Vincent into a chair.

"Now, how can I help?"

"Kurt Weber was helping me restitute a portrait by Johannes Vermeer to the Jewish family that owned it before the war. Unfortunately, he died before we could meet in person. I was told by a friend of his that you and Brigitte Vogel were frequent visitors to his gallery. I hoped you might know where he kept his paperwork so we might continue following the trail."

Max set down his cup. "By 'friend,' you must mean Helmut, the older gentleman who helped Kurt out on the weekends."

Vincent nodded, wondering whether he had just made a colossal mistake. Max's voice was filled with contempt.

"I did drop by on occasion, but I was certainly not a frequent visitor. Our fathers were good friends. Kurt does not—or I should say, did not—have any children and was quite ill. Out of respect, I would stop by now and again to see if he needed anything."

"Helmut said you often took paintings from Kurt's gallery and occasionally brought one to Kurt."

Max laughed. "The old boy does get confused, doesn't he? No, I did not take art from Kurt's gallery. His tastes were quite ordinary, and his stock would not interest my clients. I brought artwork to him so he could satisfy his few remaining clients. That is how I helped Kurt. By selling some of my art to his clients, he would get a commission on the sale," Max responded evenly, flicking a speck of dust off his pant leg.

"That was generous of you," Vincent said, realizing that Max's statement directly contradicted what Helmut had told Zelda.

Max tilted his head in acknowledgment.

"Do you know if Kurt had a storage unit, perhaps a second home, or any other place he may have stored his business paperwork?" Vincent knew Kurt had both but wanted to see how much Max knew or was willing to share.

"I'm really not certain. We weren't that close."

"Do you know who would benefit from his death—who would inherit the gallery, for example?"

Max seemed genuinely shocked. "I honestly do not know. That is an excellent question for his lawyer."

"Would Brigitte Vogel be able to help me?" Vincent asked.

Max's nostrils flared. "I doubt it. Neither of us was a frequent visitor, as Helmut claims. He is an old man. I can imagine he got the days confused, and it seemed to him that we stopped by more often than we did."

"How do you know Brigitte Vogel?"

Max's eyes narrowed. "There aren't that many art dealers in Munich who trade in twentieth-century paintings. We know each other from art fairs and work together on occasion."

"So you aren't involved in a relationship and only know each other professionally?" Vincent was surprised the inspector had gotten it so wrong. It was only the second small discrepancy, but it did stick out.

"That is correct," he said through gritted teeth.

"Great. Thank you." Vincent started to rise when a thought made him sit down again. "I don't want to put you on the spot, but I do have to ask. I did some research into Weber's background and was surprised to see links between your families—the Vogels, Webers, and several others."

Max bristled. "If you are here to talk about that ridiculous looting art program—"

Vincent threw his hands up in the air. "No, sorry, the police made clear that there is no truth to rumors about such a network still existing. But it is a fact that your paternal grandfather did work for Hitler as one of his art advisors."

"Yes, it is a dark page in our family history." Max seethed. "Do you have any idea how much that stain has tarnished my parents' lives? Everyone conveniently forgets that after the war, my grandfather helped the Allies restitute stolen art to their owners! My family has given millions to charities benefiting victims of the Nazis' atrocities. We practice due diligence in our galleries. In fact, I have personally discovered and returned three pieces of looted art brought into my gallery by unsuspecting owners. Yet whenever rumors about this network surface, we all go through the wringer. I feel as if I must spend my life trying to right the wrongs of a man I never met."

Vincent held his palms up. "I'm sorry to have brought up such a sensitive topic."

"You have no idea. If anyone is a bad seed, it was Bruno Weber. He's the one who was convicted of selling a forgery. It appears his son is as bad as his father. Did you know that Kurt sold looted paintings to three Swiss dealers last week? I wouldn't be surprised if they turn out to be Bruno's forgeries that he was trying to pass off on them."

"I did hear about that case."

"Good." Max sucked in a deep breath and rose. "Now, if you don't have any more questions, I have an appointment with a client."

"Thank you for your time," Vincent said and stood with him.

Max watched Vincent amble down the street, obviously taking his time so as to see his next appointment. In fact, his client was not due for more than an hour, but Max wanted time to change his clothes before the social media star and his entourage arrived. His suit was dusty from searching through Kurt's house. The man should have kept a tidier home.

Before he raced home to shower and change, he had one quick task to take care of. After the private detective rounded the corner, Max picked up his phone and called Inspector Bauer.

28

Kernel of Truth

"Are we good friends? No, I wouldn't say that about Kurt Weber," Brigitte Vogel said, shaking her head in emphasis. She sat perched on the edge of her chair, a cup of tea in hand.

Vincent had headed over to her gallery as soon as he was done with Max Wolf. He only hoped Max hadn't already called and prepped her.

On the surface, Brigitte had graciously answered all of his questions about Kurt Weber and Neue Gallery without hesitation. Yet Vincent felt as if she were holding information back. Specifically what or why, he couldn't say.

"But you did visit his gallery often? Or was his friend wrong about that?"

She set the cup down, the clinking porcelain mirroring her irritation. "I stopped by once a month. Kurt was healthy enough to run his gallery, but he hadn't kept up with marketing, and his business was slowly dying. He still had regular clients who wanted to buy the kinds of artwork I specialize in."

"Did you also buy art from Kurt to resell to your clients?"

Brigitte looked as if she had eaten a lemon. "God, no. He had terrible taste in art."

"So you brought artwork to Kurt that he sold on to his clients—I assume at a profit?" Vincent asked. The incredulity in his voice was evident.

"I did him a favor by not working directly with his clients. My gallery is quite successful, and I didn't sell enough to Kurt for it to be a problem."

"Still, that is very generous of you."

Brigitte shrugged. "My grandmother was a good friend of his father. It's the least I could do."

"Funny, Max Wolf said the same thing." Listening to Brigitte gave him déjà vu. Perhaps Max had gotten in touch with her before Vincent arrived.

Brigitte scrunched up her nose. "Yes, well, the art market in Munich is small now, but it was tiny in the 1930s. I think most gallery owners were friendly back then." She began to rise. "Is there anything else I can do for you?"

"Yes, there is. Do you know where Kurt's friend Helmut is?"

"I believe he lives in the same neighborhood as Kurt's gallery." Brigitte reacted visibly to his name, almost shuddering, making the hair on the back of Vincent's neck bristle.

"I mean, do you know where Helmut is now? He disappeared the same night Kurt died. Helmut and Kurt were good friends, and I hope to talk to him. Do you have any idea of where he could be?"

"He disappeared? That's odd. I had no idea."

Vincent had tried calling Helmut repeatedly and stopped by his apartment several times, but the man was unreachable. He thought that Zelda was one of the last to speak with Helmut before he left Munich, but based on Brigitte's agitated reaction, perhaps Zelda wasn't the very last.

"Max Wolf said you had more contact with Helmut than he did, so that's why I am asking." At the mention of Max's name, Brigitte began to blush. "What exactly is your relationship with Mr. Wolf?" Vincent pressed.

"I don't see what our friendship has to do with your investigation. And as far as Helmut goes, he was a quiet, old man who I exchanged pleasantries with, not someone I got to know intimately."

That's not what Helmut says, Vincent thought.

Max also pretended that he barely knew Brigitte, yet she referred to him as a friend. It caught his attention, this first contradiction, however small. Before he could continue, his phone began vibrating in his pocket, alerting him to a missed call. He ignored the distraction when Brigitte's phone began to ring, as well.

"Excuse me, I need to take this," she said, and Vincent swore he saw relief in her eyes.

He pulled his phone out of his pocket when she crossed to her study and answered her landline. There were three missed calls, all from Inspector Bauer. When it began to ring in his hand, he answered, certain the policeman had new information concerning Weber's death or the missing artwork.

"Yes, this is Vincent."

"Vincent de Graaf. I have received a harassment complaint from Max Wolf."

He bent over and covered his mouth with one hand, hoping Brigitte couldn't hear the conversation. "What do you mean? We spoke this morning, but it was a civil conversation. In fact, he was quite polite and forthcoming."

"He claims you pestered him about his family's Nazi past, specifically what I asked you not to do. He and his parents contribute heavily to many important charities. I thought you understood that this is a sensitive subject."

"I gather," Vincent responded.

"I am not going to file this claim officially but will leave it at a verbal warning. I have to ask you to contact his lawyer if you have any more questions."

Vincent wanted to scream out in frustration. Why was Max turning their harmless conversation into a big deal? Instead, Vincent kept his tone level. "Certainly, Inspector. I understand."

When he hung up, Brigitte was standing next to her front door. "That was my lawyer. He said I am not to speak with you unless he is present."

"Of course. I'll get out of your hair." Vincent knew there was no point in continuing this conversation with her legal aid present. She wouldn't tell him anything useful, anyway.

As he strolled up the street, Vincent wondered why Max was so upset. Was it simply that he was tired of being questioned about his family's Nazi past? Or was there more to the story? Vincent didn't like being told what to do. He would have to spend more time researching the connections between the Vogel, Wolf, and Weber families. Perhaps there was a kernel of truth to the often-told lies about the Nazis' art looting program.

29

Tickle Torture

Zelda snuggled up against Jacob as they spooned in their hotel room bed. "What a great day," she murmured in his ear.

"It really was," he mumbled softly while kissing her cheek.

Their trip to Neuschwanstein Castle was the perfect day trip from Munich. Not only was the castle itself a magical place, the drive through the Bavarian Alps was incredible. On the way back to Munich, they had stopped off at two smaller, though no less extraordinary, castles. Zelda liked the Schloss Linderhof most of all. Both the interior furnishings and fountain-filled gardens were spectacular.

Zelda could hardly believe that her parents' trip was coming to an end. The castle was the last major site they would see as a group, she realized with a tinge of regret. After they returned to Amsterdam, her parents would only be in town for two more nights before they had to fly home. Thankfully, they'd had plenty of time together these past two weeks to catch up and sightsee.

And it was great that they'd gotten to spend so much time with Jacob, especially considering he was taking a train back to Cologne, instead of accompanying them back to Amsterdam. She was simply grateful he had been able to take so much time off.

Tomorrow was their last full day in Munich, and they had decided on the bus ride back to split up for the afternoon so her parents could shop and Jacob could climb the old Olympic Stadium. Since Zelda was not a fan of heights, she would not be joining him, but was curious to see the old Olympic Village and surrounding park. Given that she had spent so much of their time chasing after the Vermeer, she was happy to hang out with a book for a while if that meant her partner could do something on his bucket list.

As amenable as Zelda's mom was to their splitting up for a few hours, she was insistent that they meet back up at the hotel before five o'clock.

No matter what Zelda said or did, her parents refused to tell her why it was so imperative. Jacob was no help either, as he was as close-lipped as her parents.

Is Dad finally retiring and Mom wants to celebrate it? But why here, instead of in Amsterdam? Zelda pondered. It must be because today was Jacob's last day with them.

She had been racking her brain the entire trip, trying to figure out what they had been planning behind her back. But nothing made sense. Everything she could think of was family related. So why would her parents tell Jacob about it and exclude her?

Zelda decided to try once more to get her boyfriend to reveal the secret. She started her tickle attack at his armpits before moving to his feet. "So what exactly do you have planned tomorrow evening?

"I refuse to divulge our secret, no matter how badly you torture me," he squealed, grabbing hold of her hands to stop her assault. "You are just going to have to wait." Jacob leaned down and kissed her naked skin, clearly trying to sidetrack her.

"I thought having you join us in Munich was the surprise," she whispered.

"That was part of it," he said teasingly, "but not all of it." His butterfly kisses were electrifying and most distracting.

"The fact that you are all in on it makes me incredibly nervous," she said, before pulling his mouth to hers.

30

Black Sheep

When Zelda woke up the next morning, she felt rested and happy. It wasn't until she was brushing her teeth that she thought about Vincent and the Vermeer. Had he left a message, and she didn't hear the beep?

After showering, she checked her phone, but there were no unread messages. With a little luck, they would run into each other in the breakfast hall and he could catch her up on yesterday's events. He should have met with Brigitte Vogel and Max Wolf yesterday, and Zelda couldn't wait to hear what they'd said about Kurt Weber's paperwork or the missing artwork.

When they entered the hotel's breakfast room, Zelda was thrilled to see Vincent was at the buffet filling his plate. Her parents were already seated, plates of eggs and sausages on the table before them.

"Oh, good, Vincent's already here." Zelda squeezed her boyfriend's hand. "Would you mind if I talked to him alone for a few minutes? I want to find out if he knows more about the Vermeer's authenticity. Then we'll have the rest of the day for us, okay?"

"Of course not. Take your time." He kissed her forehead before joining her parents.

When Zelda approached her boss, she could tell that he was not in a good mood simply by his slouching posture. "Good morning, Vincent. So, how did it go yesterday?"

"Not so great. I chatted with Max, then Brigitte. While I was at Brigitte's gallery, Max filed a harassment complaint with Inspector Bauer."

"What did you do?" Zelda knew that Vincent had a way of aggravating people.

"Nothing, this time. I was at Brigitte's gallery, and she had just contradicted Helmut and Max when Bauer contacted me. Now I'm not allowed to speak to her or Max without their lawyers present."

"Which means neither one will answer your questions."

"Yep."

"What did she say that contradicted Helmut and Max's accounts?"

"Max claims that they are colleagues and nothing more, yet Brigitte was acting like a schoolgirl in love when I asked about him. And Inspector Bauer also thought they were a couple. Maybe it's just a crush, but I got the feeling they are dating."

"Hmm, well, yeah, maybe they haven't been together long, and Max isn't ready to announce their relationship to the world."

"That could be it, or they have different viewpoints on their relationship. Frankly, I don't care either way, but it is an inconsistency. Oh, and both Brigitte and Max claim that they did not stop by Kurt's gallery often—as Helmut stated. And when they did, they brought work to Kurt but never took any of his art with them. Both were quite adamant about that."

"That's just odd. What does Inspector Bauer think?"

"As far as the police are concerned, Kurt Weber was an unsuccessful dealer who was playing mind games with a naïve researcher."

"I don't believe it—why would Helmut lie? He was terrified someone from this network was going to harm him as they did Kurt. That was no acting."

"Bauer called again last night. His teams visited Kurt's storage unit and two homes yesterday. They didn't find any artwork or proof that Kurt possessed a larger collection of looted masterpieces."

"We have to talk to Helmut and get him to go to the police." Zelda picked up her phone and dialed, but the call went straight to voicemail. Refusing to give up, she spoke in a frantic message, hoping he would sense her urgency and get in touch with the police before it was too late.

Vincent watched her, pursing his lips in irritation. "Zelda, this has to stop. I've talked with all of the major players except for Helmut, and there is absolutely no evidence proving Kurt Weber had a secret stash or a real Vermeer. It's all lies."

"But—" Zelda began, but her boss cut her off.

"No, listen—I don't believe this Network exists, and neither do the police. Every time a new rumor surfaces, they investigate it, yet they have never found a lead that panned out. The old Nazis are long gone, and the new generation is doing everything it can to put distance between them and their forefathers. By pursuing this lead without strong new evidence, we are just dredging up lies and rumors and calling them facts."

"Again, why would Kurt lie? He had no idea I was coming and had nothing to gain by giving me the Vermeer."

"Yes, he did—don't you see that?" Vincent shook his head in exasperation. "He told you that your timing was impeccable, correct? If anything, Kurt is the black sheep in this story, not Max and Brigitte. Yes, all of their parents were involved with the Nazis somehow or another, but many residents of Munich have Nazi ties if you look hard enough."

Zelda shook her head.

"And let's say he did have a collection stashed away," Vincent pushed. "Why would he be living like that? Where did he store the art? Who was he selling it to? I have found absolutely no proof that makes me believe Kurt Weber was anything but a liar who was trying to pull one last cruel joke on a Nazi victim before leaving this earth."

"I understand what you're saying, Vincent. But I can't let this go without talking to Helmut. You need to hear what he has to say."

"He won't return my calls and is not answering his door. That tells me he does not want us to be involved. He was Kurt's best friend—how can you be certain he wasn't lying to you, as well?"

"I hope I am never as cynical as you," Zelda said, pulling out her phone. "Helmut is the key to this mess—I know he is. Until we talk to him, it's all conjecture."

"You're wasting your time, Zelda," Vincent growled.

Zelda prayed that Helmut answered. Without his help, they were at a dead end. She was about to hang up when on the fifth ring, she heard his guttural voice say, "This is Helmut."

31

Initiating Kurt's Plan

Helmut listened to the American researcher pleading into his phone. Zelda Richardson had left several messages, all imploring him to contact the police and tell them about the Network and Kurt's collection. It wasn't right that the police assumed Kurt was burning forgeries or that he had lied to Zelda about the Vermeer's authenticity.

As much as Helmut wanted to respond to the police's allegations, he knew it was better, in the long run, to implement Kurt's plan instead.

"Patience, child," he said aloud as he deleted Zelda's last message.

It felt as if she were channeling Kurt, urging him to finish the task he promised to complete. Helmut still couldn't believe the Network's audacity. Kurt's death was no accident. He had not become so weak that he would have lost his balance so easily. And he would never have burned the Vermeer—it was real, not a fake.

If only Kurt had given him a copy of the letter he was writing to the restitution commission. His friend had shown him a rough draft when he had stopped by for strudel and to explain his plan, but it was not yet complete. Helmut tried to recollect the text from memory, but he wasn't certain of all of the names on Kurt's long list of dealers. He knew that returning the art was as important as dismantling the entire Network, which was why he assumed the letter was with the artwork and ledgers in Heidelberg. Yet he had searched the house from top to bottom after the police left, but couldn't find it anywhere. As much as he wanted to fulfill his promise to Kurt, this wasn't the Nazi era. He couldn't live with persecuting someone who may not even be involved.

Helmut rifled through the furniture in the sparsely decorated cottage one last time, wanting to be certain Kurt hadn't left any more information hidden away in a drawer or cupboard before he set his hand to re-creating Kurt's last statement. His version wouldn't roll up the entire network, but it would hopefully ensure that the artwork Bruno saved would finally be returned to its rightful owners.

Luckily, Kurt had left his father's ledgers behind with the artwork. The information they contained would enable the German authorities to couple these expensive paintings with their former owners. Even without Kurt's letter, there was enough information in the ledgers to satisfy both the media and police, Helmut realized, feeling slightly better. Not only did Bruno describe—in detail—the artwork he saved in his ledgers, but notes added later by Kurt told the police where they should look for those paintings that were sold.

Reading through those old books made Helmut realize how big of a mess he'd gotten into by saying yes. Kurt had told Helmut the basics about the Network and how Max and Brigitte's grandparents were involved, but not much about their clients. When he skimmed the old ledgers, he was scared to discover that many of the looted paintings both Bruno and Kurt sold had gone to important German citizens.

Kurt was insistent the press and police be notified simultaneously for fear the news would be swept under the rug. If he couldn't find the letter, emailing the media and police this home's location would be enough. Once they arrived, he could explain what Kurt was trying to do. It would be easier in person than via email.

Helmut walked through his family home to the back room where he and Kurt had moved all of the crates filled with artwork. After they had finished, they had stacked up empty boxes and shifted a heavy cupboard in front of the door in the hopes that any thieves would not happen upon it. Kurt was terrified of a random robber breaking in and getting lucky. The home was centrally located in the historic center and did have a security system, but the entrance was in a quiet, tree-filled square.

Helmut thought back to Kurt's enthusiasm and determination when his friend explained his plan. He finally admitted to what Helmut had suspected for years—many of Kurt's clients were knowingly buying Nazi-looted art, paintings his father had essentially stolen from Hitler. A group of morally louche dealers, still operating all over the world, actively traded in their secret collections. Kurt said the Network wouldn't let him return his father's collection, so he concocted this plan to expose them all.

Kurt's energy had inspired Helmut to say yes immediately, despite his cautious nature. He also knew his dying friend had no other choice. The Network was pervasive, and almost everyone his friend knew in Munich was involved in one way or the other.

Kurt's actions were noble—if not misguided and decades too late. Yet it wasn't his fault he had inherited this mess. At least Kurt was trying to set things right. As a way of paying his last respects to his friend, Helmut knew he had to finish what Kurt started.

Helmut looked to his phone, considering his options. It was time to initiate Kurt's plan, but he was scared that if he did, this Network would murder him, as well. Kurt mentioned that the Network's reach extended beyond the art world, but did it include the police? And if so, who? How he wished Kurt had shared with him the names of those he trusted. If he called the wrong person, the Network would dispose of him before the artwork could be recovered.

Before Helmut could decide what to do next, his phone rang. It was Zelda Richardson again, the young woman who worked for a Dutch private investigator. Helmut closed his eyes and drew in a deep breath. She was the only one who seemed to believe him. Her detective boss might be able to help him sort out this mess, and it would be good to have someone else here when the police arrived. They were less likely to confiscate the artwork and deny its existence to the press if there were reliable witnesses present. And as much as Kurt wanted him to inform the international and local media, Helmut felt foolish contacting a television station and reporting the art's presence. He wondered whether anyone would even believe him.

Besides, he loved his life in Munich. It was where he and his wife had spent their best days. Every walk around the city reminded him of her. He could never leave, but if he were interviewed by German television about the looted art, he would have to flee for his life just as Kurt had tried to do. No, it would be better to have the detective deal with the press and police. In fact, he could wait to call anyone until after the detective arrived; he would be more used to dealing with the police and would know what to say.

Helmut answered the phone, hoping by doing so, he was fulfilling his friend's desires as well as saving his own life.

"This is Helmut." As expected, it took Zelda a moment to recover from the shock before she began speaking.

"I'm so glad I caught you. Have you heard my messages?"

"Yes, I know what you want me to do. I have the artwork Kurt's father saved and am ready to hand it over to the police. But I cannot go to the authorities just yet. I need the help of your boss, the investigator," Helmut said in halting English.

"Of course. I'm here with Vincent de Graaf. I'm putting you on speakerphone."

"This is Vincent. Where are you, Helmut?"

"In Heidelberg, at my family's home. The artwork is here. I have never dealt with the police before and would feel better if you were here when they arrived," Helmut said, struggling to find the right words. "Can you come to the house?"

"How many paintings are we talking about?" Vincent asked.

"More than three hundred."

"And these are all paintings Kurt's father saved during World War II?"

"Yes, all of them." Helmut was relieved that Vincent had said "saved" instead of "stole."

"What is the address?"

"Bienenstrasse, number 11." Helmut felt such relief, unburdening himself in this way. Once the detective and Zelda arrived, they could call the police together. Or perhaps Interpol was the best choice. He would let the detective decide. It would take him time to drive over from Munich, giving Helmut a chance to finish searching for the letter and write up a list of the most influential media in case the detective wished to contact them.

The excitement in Zelda's voice was audible. "We can leave right away. Or should we—"

His ringing doorbell interrupted their conversation. Helmut mumbled under his breath.

"Was that your doorbell?" Zelda asked.

"Yes," he said, irritated as it began to ring again. "It's probably my neighbor bringing me another stew. She says that I need to fatten up." He laughed. "Let me get rid of her. I'll be right back."

Helmut set the phone down before Zelda could respond and walked to the door.

When someone began knocking on the door, Helmut called out, "Okay, I'm coming."

Helmut looked through the peephole, expecting to see his older neighbor. Instead, a young man in an expensive suit stood with his back to the door. Parked behind him was a black SUV, and standing next to the car was a large man dressed in black.

Helmut cleared his throat and then called out through the closed door, "Yes? Who's there?"

When the man turned to face the peephole, Helmut stepped back in shock. It was Max Wolf, one of the two young gallery owners Kurt often worked with. But Kurt had told him that he wanted to move the artwork here because no one in the Network knew this place existed.

"I'm looking for Kurt Weber. He's not answering his phone or his door in Munich. Is he here with you? My buyer is getting impatient, so if Kurt wants to make a deal, he needs to get in touch with me right away."

Oh, no, Helmut thought, *this young man must not know Kurt is dead.* He unlocked the door and opened it a crack.

Max smiled as he slammed the door into Helmut, knocking him hard onto the tiled floor.

"What is the meaning of this?" Helmut asked as he felt his head. Everything hurt. He moved his hip gingerly, fearing the worst.

The large man dressed in black entered his home, then Max closed the door behind them before Helmut thought to scream for help. The young gallery owner dragged him by the collar into the living room, away from the front door, then stood over him. "Where is the artwork?"

"What are you talking about?" Helmut was having trouble focusing his eyes, seeing double of the man.

"Don't be coy. I found Kurt's letter and know what he was planning to do. The artwork is not his to give away."

"Help!" Helmut yelled anyway, hoping someone would hear him despite the thick walls and quiet streets. Suddenly, he remembered the phone. "Zelda, help. It's Max Wolf, and he's here in Heidelberg!" Helmut screamed, hoping she could hear him.

Max followed his gaze, quickly spotting the phone. He hung up the call, then crushed it under his foot. "No one can help you now, Helmut. Cover him," Max said to his associate, who pulled on a pair of gloves, then took a gun out of his jacket.

Max quickly walked through the house, and soon found the crates stacked up in the back bedroom. Helmut could hear him opening several. When Max returned to the living room, he was grinning from ear to ear.

"Change of plans. This needs to look like a suicide."

Before Max's words could register, the large man wrapped Helmut's hand around the gun, placed it to his temple, and then pulled the trigger.

32

A Dream Come True

Zelda was so excited that she was practically dancing. Helmut had actually answered and confirmed that Kurt's artwork was real and in Heidelberg. And he wanted Vincent and her to help him reveal its existence to the world! It was a dream come true.

Vincent and Zelda heard the phone being set down. Helmut must have placed it on his couch or a soft chair because the sound was now muffled.

Vincent covered the phone with his hand. "If Helmut is telling the truth, and Kurt did leave hundreds of looted paintings behind, then Inspector Bauer will have to investigate his death, and the possibility that someone killed Kurt in order to keep him quiet."

The sounds of rising voices caused Zelda to hold the phone closer to her ear. "Is Helmut arguing with someone?"

Vincent put his finger to his lips, listening intently. Zelda did the same. It sounded like Helmut was pleading with someone. Or was he angry? It was hard to tell. After a moment's silence, a scuffle ensued, and it sounded like Helmut was shouting. Then the phone was disconnected.

"What just happened? Did someone just hurt Helmut?" Zelda cried. She redialed, but there was no answer. "We have to help him."

Vincent sighed and shook his head. "I should have known better. He's playing us, just like Kurt tried to. He probably pulled a chair across the room and hung up the phone so that we would rush to Heidelberg."

"Then why did he tell us where the artwork is at?" Zelda pushed.

"If it's even there. He probably just wants to lead us on a fool's errand."

Zelda put her hands on her hips and glared at him. "Wait a second, we finally get ahold of Helmut, he confirms the existence of Kurt's collection of looted artwork, and you still don't believe him?"

"No, I don't. And I won't until I see the artwork. It's that simple."

"What's wrong with you?" she shrieked.

Zelda's mother had been watching from their breakfast table but came rushing over when her daughter became hysterical. "What's going on? I thought you were done with this Vermeer business."

"It's not that simple, Mom. We finally got in touch with Helmut. He is the only person who can verify Kurt's story, and it sounds like someone hurt him while we were on the line."

"Whoa, I wouldn't go that far. We don't know what happened," Vincent added.

Her mother went white. "Oh my God, you have to call the police."

"I'm not calling anyone until I know what is really going on," Vincent said, his tone resolute. "I don't trust Kurt or Helmut."

"We have to go to Heidelberg. What if he was telling the truth, and someone is there stealing the artwork as we speak?" Zelda pleaded.

"Are you crazy?" Debbie cried. "You just said you heard someone getting harmed, and now you want to go to their house and see what's happening? Call the Heidelberg police; that's what they are there for."

"If we do, then we may never know if Kurt Weber's art is really there or not," Vincent said. "There is no way Inspector Bauer will let me get involved. I upset too many important German citizens for him to allow that to happen."

"Don't you dare drag my daughter into this," Debbie snarled. "You're the detective, so figure it out yourself."

"Mom! I know you are worried about my safety, but I want to know if the Vermeer is there, as much as Vincent does. Maybe more. I need to go with him."

"What about our plans tonight? Where is Heidelberg, anyway?" Debbie asked.

Before Zelda could respond, Vincent said, "As much as I would love for you to join me, maybe it is better if I go alone. It is a four-and-a-half-hour drive."

Zelda looked at her watch. It was just after eight in the morning. "If we leave now, we'll have two hours to sort this out before I need to come back. I'll take a taxi back if I need to, but I am not missing this chance to see Kurt's collection. Besides, you haven't met Helmut, but I have. He might not trust you enough to let you inside."

"If he's even there," Vincent countered.

"Zelda, I can see by the look in your eye that you have already made up your mind," her mother said. "But before you leave, you really need to tell Jacob what you are planning on doing."

"Of course," Zelda responded and looked to her boyfriend, who had sprung up at the mention of his name and was moving to join them.

"Do you really think the missing art is in Heidelberg?" Jacob asked as soon as he had crossed over to them.

"I do," Zelda replied quickly.

"Then let's get going." Jacob turned to Vincent. "I take it there's room for all of us in your car?"

Vincent nodded, but his tense expression made clear that he was not pleased to have company. "Zelda, this is nothing more than a wild-goose chase. Are you certain this is the way you want to spend your last day in Munich?"

"I am. If we don't go, I will always wonder if Kurt and Helmut were telling us the truth."

"And our dinner plans?" Debbie pushed.

Before Zelda could respond, Jacob said, "It will work out."

That was apparently good enough for her mother. "Okay, well, good luck," Debbie said. "I hope you find what you are looking for, Zelda."

She pulled her mother in for a hug. "Thanks, Mom. Me, too."

33

One Problem Solved

While his bodyguard positioned Helmut's body on the couch, Max considered what to do next. *Just when you get one problem solved, another appears,* he thought. Helmut was talking to Zelda Richardson when he arrived—the assistant of Vincent de Graaf, the Dutch detective who was so keen to find Weber's Vermeer. The last thing they needed was to have him show up in Heidelberg and find the crates.

Had Helmut already told him where the art was? Possibly. Because he had crushed Helmut's phone, he had no way of knowing how long their conversation was. Even if Helmut had given Zelda this address, it was a long drive from Munich. He had plenty of time to solve this current crisis. It wouldn't be enough just to move the artwork to a more secure location. He had to set up a scene that would make the Dutch detective lose interest in this case.

Think, man. Max closed his eyes and concentrated on his choices, quickly calculating the time and risk involved. After pondering his options, a smile cracked his lips.

If Vincent got what he came for, would he leave well enough alone? Max had little choice but to assume he would.

Max had sent Brigitte to Mannheim this morning, thinking he might need a scapegoat if Kurt's artwork was indeed in Heidelberg. Mannheim was only a half-hour drive away from Helmut's home, meaning she could get to his house quickly, if need be. If the police had already been tipped off, he could send Brigitte over to take the fall. Protecting the Network was more important than any one member.

But Helmut's presence changed everything. With the right staging, the whole problem would go away, and he wouldn't have to implicate Brigitte. Yet he would need her help. Would she agree to cooperate? It would take some convincing and cost him quite a bit of art, but he would make her see that his idea was sound, and the only one guaranteed to get Vincent out of Germany.

First things first, he had to figure out how he was going to get all of this artwork to his home in Walldorf. It was close by and spacious enough, yet there were far too many crates to move them all with his SUV.

Max turned to his associate. "We are going to need a moving truck. You should be able to rent one in town."

His bodyguard nodded in confirmation, then set off to accomplish his task.

Max found an old typewriter in a spare bedroom he could use to craft Helmut's final words. If the police and Vincent de Graaf believed what he wrote, both would consider this case closed. But first, it was time to call Brigitte.

34

Is It True?

Shortly after Max's bodyguard returned with a rental van, Brigitte knocked on Helmut's door. "Is it true?" she asked as she rushed into the house, but one look at Helmut's body and the dark hole in his forehead tempered her enthusiasm.

Max pulled her past Helmut's corpse toward the back bedroom. "Yes, it's true. There are hundreds of paintings in these crates."

"Have you checked to see what's inside?"

"No, but Kurt left behind his father's ledgers. From what I have read so far, it is exquisite and will fill in both of our collections nicely."

Brigitte raised an eyebrow.

"We have one problem left to resolve before we can leave with the art. That Dutch detective doesn't seem to be giving up on his client's Vermeer. I think I know how we can fix this, but I will need your help."

Brigitte nodded. "Go on."

"We are going to make Helmut our scapegoat and hopefully distract de Graaf from discovering the truth."

"What do you need from me?"

"The Vermeer."

Brigitte looked up at him, puzzled. "Why do you want it? De Graaf thinks it was a fake that burned up in Kurt's fireplace. Isn't it wiser to let him believe that it's true?"

Max smiled. "I have a better idea."

After moving the crates to his home in Walldorf, Max poured a glass of whiskey for them all.

"*Prost* to Kurt," he said with a laugh.

Brigitte and his bodyguard clinked glasses with him. They were all seated around the dining room table inside one of the five homes Max owned in Germany. His father had taught him the importance of spreading his financial risks and considered real estate to be an excellent investment.

"Let's take a look at the ledgers and see what Kurt left us, shall we?" he said, his tone light and frivolous. Based on the few crates that he had already opened, Max expected this collection to be worth several million dollars.

Brigitte downed her whiskey, then grabbed her keys. "They are in my truck. I'll be right back." She gave Max a peck on the cheek, then walked out to the driveway. She soon returned with four thick volumes.

"I think you'll be pleased, Max. His father really did have a fantastic eye for quality." Brigitte had flipped through them whenever she took a break from moving crates into the truck. She opened the oldest book, dated 1942, and began pointing to the names of artists she admired.

"Where is the other ledger?" Max asked.

Brigitte's smile froze. "There were only four, right?"

"No. Kurt left five in the bedroom with the crates. I am certain of it. I put all five onto the kitchen table for your perusal."

Brigitte paled. "Oh, no. I must have left the other one behind."

"You fool! The police cannot find it there. That will blow our entire plan apart and rekindle interest in our business."

"I'll go get the ledger," Brigitte responded immediately. "It's my fault. I'll fix this."

Max looked at his watch. It had taken them four hours to move all of the crates to Walldorf. If Helmut had told Vincent where the art was, he was probably pulling into Heidelberg right about now.

"Watch out for that detective." He turned to his bodyguard. "Why don't you go with her, just in case."

Brigitte squeezed Max's hand. "I'm so sorry. We'll take care of it. Don't worry."

"I hope so."

As Brigitte rushed out of the house, Max held his bodyguard back. "If that Dutch detective is there, recovering the book is of the utmost importance. What happens to Brigitte is secondary."

"Understood."

35

A Quick Trip to Heidelberg

Traffic between Munich and Heidelberg was horrible. Zelda and Jacob sat in the back seat holding hands, too keyed up to chitchat. Vincent, apparently lost in his own thoughts, seemed content to play chauffeur. Only when they turned off of the busy Autobahn did he speak up.

"We're here."

Zelda startled at his voice, then looked out the window, pleasantly surprised by the town's location along a lovely river. However, the industrial buildings and concrete boxes dominating the view were less enchanting.

"Is this it?"

"Not quite. This is the new town. Old Town is around the next bend."

"I didn't realize you had been to Heidelberg before," Zelda said.

"I dated a girl attending university here for a few years." Vincent grinned as he made eye contact with her in the rearview mirror. "If I remember correctly, most of the Old Town is a pedestrian zone. We'll have to find a parking garage and walk over. Could you see if there's one close to Helmut's home?"

"Sure." She checked her phone's map. "There are two options, both practically next to his house."

"Excellent," Vincent replied and relaxed into his seat.

They drove through the modern city center before navigating onto a street running parallel to the Neckar River. The homes seemed to age with every foot they traveled, and soon they were driving alongside stately buildings and houses made of marble and stone. Many were constructed from a gorgeous red stone that Zelda had never seen before. More impressive was its position; the historic center seemed to be built into the base of a forest-covered mountain called Königstuhl, according to the map on Zelda's phone.

She gazed up the streets as they drove past. All seemed to go straight up the mountain and ended in the thick forest crowning Heidelberg.

"It is pretty romantic," Jacob said as he craned his neck to better see the glorious old homes and medieval city center.

"It's too bad that we don't have more time to sightsee. Maybe we take a quick walk through the old center after we meet with Helmut?" Zelda offered.

Her boyfriend chuckled. "Sounds good to me, but if Kurt Weber's artwork really is inside his home, we might have other priorities. And I did promise your mother that we would be back before five."

"You make a good point. I better call Helmut and let him know we are almost there," Zelda said, hoping the older man would finally answer his phone.

"You can try, but I bet he's halfway to Berlin by now," Vincent replied.

"He didn't lie to me. There was no reason for him to do so," Zelda said, determination in her voice. She refused to believe that Helmut and Kurt had been stringing her along this whole time. Yet, both of the calls she had made on the way over had gone straight to voicemail. The traffic had delayed them so much that it was already two in the afternoon, meaning she and Jacob needed to head back to Munich in an hour. Despite the brevity of their visit, to Zelda, the chance to see the three hundred and fifty-seven paintings Bruno Weber saved from Hitler's grasp was worth every minute of the ride. She just hoped that Helmut was home and that there was a reasonable explanation for the scuffle they had heard through the phone.

Before she could respond, her telephone beeped. "Take the next right and we should see the entrance to the first parking garage."

Vincent did as directed, and moments later they were driving into a parking garage built under several old homes.

After they exited and had oriented themselves, Vincent said, "Helmut's house should be further up, on the right."

The closer they came to the historic Old Town that Heidelberg was famous for, the busier and prettier it became. The colorful homes were built close together in a maze of narrow streets. An ancient brick bridge with a bulbous old gate on one end stretched across the river, looking like something from a fairy tale. Boat cruises full of day-trippers plied the busy waterway. Busloads of tourists were being dropped off or picked up on the only road running through this section of town, making it even more chaotic.

High up on the mountain was an enormous castle made of a honey-brown stone. It seemed to emerge from a massive outcrop that loomed over the historic center. Sheer stone ramparts, several stories tall, held the immense stone structure in place.

"Oh, wow, that's beautiful." Zelda slowed her pace.

"Impressive, isn't it? That's Heidelberg Castle. The views from up there are extraordinary."

"How do you get there?" Jacob asked.

Zelda could see hundreds of tourists standing on the ramparts, but the entire structure seemed to be surrounded by greenery.

"There's an access road that leads around the back, but most tourists use the *Bergbahn*."

"The what?"

"It's a funicular, a type of train that goes straight up the mountainside all the way up to the top. It's a Swiss invention if I'm not mistaken."

Zelda strained her eyes, trying to see it through the trees. She had just caught sight of a trio of train carriages riding perpendicular up the mountain face when Vincent called out, "Here's Helmut's street."

Adrenaline began coursing through her veins. "It's number eleven."

They turned onto a quiet, tree-filled square. It was almost surreal finding this serene oasis in this middle of the busy center. Helmut's home was quite large compared to its neighbors and appeared to be older. The deep-blue façade topped by shiny black tiles was unusual. Most of the homes they had passed were painted in muted reds and yellows.

When Vincent knocked, the door creaked open. "Uh-oh. That's not good." He put a finger to his lips, then whispered, "Wait here."

Zelda and Jacob exchanged tense glances, happy to do as Vincent asked. Her boss crept inside and was gone several excruciating minutes. An older neighbor returned home, and a group of lost tourists wandered through the square, but no one seemed to notice Zelda and Jacob admiring the trees filled with singing birds.

Vincent popped his head outside minutes later. "No one is here. You can come in."

When Zelda looked into the living room, she stifled a scream and glared at her boss. Helmut was on the couch, a gun in his hand and a hole in his head.

"Well, there is no living soul inside," he clarified.

"Oh, poor Helmut. Who did this to you?"

Vincent pulled on gloves, then picked up a typed letter lying next to Helmut. "It looks like he did it to himself. It's in German. I'll translate."

Zelda felt sicker the further he read. Not only did Helmut admit to accidentally killing Kurt in a fit of rage, the letter also clarified that the Vermeer was the only painting that Bruno Weber had saved from the Nazis. Kurt had lied about having more because he wanted to feel important. When Kurt told him what he was planning on doing, they fought, and Helmut accidentally pushed him down the stairs. Afterwards, Helmut burned several worthless paintings to confuse the police. Now that his friend was gone, the guilt was too much to bear. Ending his own life was his only way out.

Even though the gun was in his hand, Zelda had trouble accepting both the letter and Helmut's suicidal tendencies. "I don't believe it. Why would he go to so much trouble to lead us here if he was going to kill himself? The Network must be behind this."

"What network, Zelda? Helmut admits in his letter that he killed Kurt. Case closed. And there are no crates hidden away; I already checked the house. This is the only painting here. Kurt must have been lying to you about there being more art. It really looks like it was all a cruel hoax."

"I don't know," Zelda said doggedly. "It does sound like the Vermeer is real."

"Maybe. If this is a genuine Vermeer, then Roelf's family will get it back, thanks to this letter."

"Shouldn't we call the police now?" Jacob asked. "I know you want to recover the artwork, but a man is dead. We can't just take the painting and leave him here. In fact, we really shouldn't really be inside the house and touching stuff. I think we should go back outside to wait for them to arrive."

"Before we call the police, I want to take a quick look around the house. I've had a few run-ins with the Munich police and suspect they won't let us back inside, once their officers arrive."

"I'm with Jacob on this one," Zelda said as she took her boyfriend's hand. "You do what you need to do, but we are going to go back outside and call them."

"I better get a move on, then," Vincent said as he turned towards the hallway leading to the back of the house.

Zelda and Jacob shrugged at each other, then turned in the opposite direction, towards the front door. As she and Jacob passed the kitchen, a thick, old book resting on a table caught her eye. Something about the cover made her steps slow as she craned her neck to better read the cover.

"Does that say 1940-1942?" Zelda mumbled.

"What did you say?" Vincent piped up before crossing over to the book she was now pointing at.

With a gloved hand, he gently lifted the cover. As he read the first page, a low whistle escaped his lips. "This looks to be Bruno Weber's gallery ledger for 1940 through 1942."

"Are you serious?" Jacob replied, his mouth agape.

Before Vincent's words could register in Zelda's mind, the front door burst open in an explosion of wooden splinters. She looked at the shattered doorframe in confusion as a beefy man as wide as a refrigerator burst inside, his gun drawn.

He waved his pistol at Vincent and Jacob, motioning for them to back up against the wall before leveling his gun at her. "Put the book down and get against the wall."

Zelda did as she was told. After all three had stepped away from the table, the stranger grabbed the book and sprinted back outside.

"What just happened?" Zelda shrieked. Vincent running after the large man spurred her into action. She tore after her boss, Jacob on her heels.

The stranger jumped into the passenger side of a sports car that immediately pulled out into traffic once he was inside. Or tried to. A large touring bus chose that moment to stop and let a group of tourists disembark. As Zelda, Jacob, and Vincent approached the car, both the driver and passenger sprung out of the vehicle and ran off in opposite directions.

"That's Brigitte Vogel!" Vincent cried out as he pointed to the car's driver. The three froze momentarily as they watched the pair sprint away.

"You two go after Brigitte, and I'll follow the big guy," Vincent said, then rushed after his prey, running along the river in the direction of the new town.

Zelda and Jacob followed Brigitte into the maze of streets crisscrossing the historic center. The roads were so clogged with tourists that Zelda could barely make out the cobblestones under their feet. Brigitte ran ahead as if her life depended on it, but groups of tourists standing still to snap photos of the quaint homes or flower-filled balconies blocked her way.

Zelda dodged a large group led by a flag-waving tour guide, determined to catch up to Brigitte. There were so many people, and Brigitte was so short that Zelda momentarily lost sight of her target in the thick crowds.

Jacob must not have been having much luck either, because he jumped up onto the edge of a fountain to better see over the crowds.

"She just took a right-hand turn, around that building!" he called out.

Zelda tore after her, pushing through the masses instead of politely trying to find a way around. She couldn't let Brigitte get away. Was she in Heidelberg to steal the artwork Helmut had taken? Why was that ledger on Helmut's table? Did they include entries related to the Vermeer, or even reveal more looted artwork, as Kurt claimed there was?

Zelda made it to the corner in record time. When she rounded the building, she froze momentarily, astonished by the sight before her. A golden statue of the Virgin Mary holding her son tight stood in the center of a small square surrounded by beautiful old buildings. The castle was so close it seemed to loom over them. She scanned the crowd and saw Brigitte race past the statue and up a small hill, then around another corner.

"She went right again," Zelda panted as Jacob rushed by her.

He slowed down. "Are you okay?"

"I'm fine—don't slow down on my account!"

When Zelda caught up, she was shocked to see a modern concrete parking structure just behind the historical buildings. Two streets wound around it and went up the hill. On the left was a set of stairs that went straight up the mountain and disappeared into the trees. According to the sign, it led to the castle. Brigitte was nowhere to be seen.

Jacob stood in the center of the road, looking between the staircase and street.

"I don't know which way she went," he yelled when she jogged into view.

Zelda sprinted past the garage to get a better look at the street when a large poster caught her eye. This wasn't just a parking structure; it was also the first stop of the *Bergbahn* Vincent had mentioned. Was Brigitte trying to escape that way? Zelda rushed inside and over to the entrance. A gate held those without tickets back, but through it, she could see the long line of passengers waiting to enter the three train carriages pulling into the station. Brigitte was one of them.

She ran back and grabbed Jacob's hand before pulling him towards the ticket counter. "Two tickets, please."

"Certainly. Enjoy your ride," the attendant said as he buzzed open the gate.

When they joined the queue, Zelda was quite thankful that the snaking line made it difficult for Brigitte to see her. It took her fellow passengers forever to shuffle into the carriages that would take them up the mountain. Zelda hoped there was room enough for all of them. When the doors began to beep, warning they were about to close automatically, she grabbed Jacob's hand again and whipped them around the older couple before her, springing into the last carriage moments before the doors closed.

The cars were not attached, so Zelda couldn't try to sneak up on Brigitte during the ride. Instead, she had to hope that they could get a jump on her once they stopped.

She craned her neck from her seated position, trying in vain to locate Brigitte without drawing attention to herself. Just as she spotted her prey in the carriage before them, her phone vibrated in her pocket. "This is Zelda."

"Where are you?" Vincent asked.

"In the *Bergbahn*. Brigitte's in another carriage."

"Okay. I'll take the stairs and meet you at the castle."

"Did you catch the big guy?"

"No, he stole a scooter and I lost him. See you at the top."

It took several minutes to get to their next stop. With nothing left to do, Zelda gazed outside, doing her best to enjoy the extraordinary views their perpendicular train's windows offered as it slowly rose up the hillside. If only her stomach wouldn't stop clenching anytime her eyes gazed down the steep drop. She had never experienced anything quite like it before; it was only too bad her fear of heights meant she couldn't relax and enjoy it.

After their train carriages entered the first station, Jacob and Zelda scooted down in their seats and lowered their heads, hoping that Brigitte would not see them as she exited the funicular. After Brigitte walked past their carriage, Zelda popped up, hoping to follow stealthily behind. Unfortunately, she jumped onto the foot of an older tourist who began loudly scolding Zelda for not watching where she was walking. The commotion drew Brigitte's attention to her presence.

"She's getting away!" Zelda screamed to Jacob when Brigitte tore out of the *Bergbahn* station. They raced to catch up, but she was already heading down the staircase leading back down to Old Town. Zelda began to swear, when Brigitte suddenly raced back up the staircase. *Vincent must be close,* Zelda realized. Help was on its way.

When Brigitte skipped up the last steps and raced toward the castle's entrance, Zelda and Jacob ran after her, frantic to catch up. There were so many tourists milling about that Zelda quickly lost sight of her. She jogged around the ten-foot-wide rampant covered in grass and ancient trees, Jacob right behind her. On the left was a sheer drop-off to the city center. On the right was a deep, waterless moat, and next to that was the entrance to the castle. Only a low stone wall kept tourists from tumbling to their deaths.

They stopped to look around, hoping to catch sight of her, when Jacob screamed, "There she is!"

Brigitte was on the other side of the waterless moat, pushing past the ticket checkers at the castle's main entrance as she ran at top speed into the ancient ruin. When one employee grabbed her walkie-talkie and began speaking angrily into it, Zelda assumed the woman was calling security.

If she wanted to talk to Brigitte, she had to act fast.

She and Jacob circled back to the entrance and followed Brigitte's example, running at top speed through the entrance gate and past the employees attempting to block their path.

Once they were through the gate, Zelda paused momentarily, taking in the enormous ruin before her.

What looked like a complete castle from the city center far below was actually the shell of what once was. The outer walls, heavily decorated with life-size statues of regal knights wearing puffy pants, still stood, but the rest of the building was gone.

Vincent, charging through the entrance gates, caught Zelda's attention.

"Which way did she go?" her boss yelled out.

"I'm not sure," Zelda answered as she and Jacob ran towards him.

To their left was a ramp leading into the bowels of the castle with a sign pointing down, advertising the presence of the large wine vat called the Great Heidelberg Tun. Straight ahead was a tiny entrance to what appeared to be a terrace overlooking the river. The small, rounded opening in the thick stone wall perfectly framed a majestic view of the valley below. Zelda chose the barrel and raced inside, Jacob close on her heels. Vincent ran toward the terrace.

Brigitte was not admiring one of Europe's largest remaining wine barrels, meaning there was only one place she could be. Screams caused Zelda to run back toward the terrace, ducking her head to avoid hitting the hard stone entrance.

When she and Jacob entered the terrace, she saw Vincent had Brigitte cornered. While he yelled questions at her, Brigitte took tiny steps backward.

In her effort to get away from the detective, she was coming dangerously close to the edge.

"Why were you at Helmut's home? Why did Max's bodyguard steal the ledger and not the art? Is the Vermeer a forgery? Is Max Wolf involved, as well?"

Vincent kept pressing her for answers, but she didn't respond. Instead, she looked around frantically, searching for any way out. When Vincent lunged for her arm, Brigitte automatically leaned back, stumbling over the low stone wall. Her eyes widened to saucers as she began to fall.

"No!" Vincent yelled. He tried to grab her hand but was not fast enough.

Brigitte's screams as she tumbled to her death were heart-wrenching.

Zelda and Jacob raced to the edge, careful not to lose their balance. Brigitte's body lay crumpled on the road below, a circle of tourists already surrounding her.

36

Start Apologizing

After the officers responding to Brigitte Vogel's death had interviewed them, Vincent, Jacob, and Zelda headed back to Helmut's house, which was now swarming with police. It took Vincent quite a while to explain to the lead investigator why he and Zelda had traveled to Heidelberg. When he mentioned the looted art they'd expected to find, the inspector stopped him.

"All we have found was the Vermeer in the living room. There are no indications that there was a large quantity of artwork stored here," the policeman said.

"Did you question the neighbors? If Brigitte removed hundreds of paintings from this house earlier today, somebody must have noticed it."

"None of the neighbors reported seeing anything unusual happening today."

Vincent momentarily lost his cool. "Nothing unusual? A man is dead!" He glared at the ground until he regained his composure. "The Vermeer belonged to my client, Roelf Konig. That's what brought us to Munich and in contact with Helmut. His friend, an art dealer named Kurt Weber, had promised to return it to its rightful owner, but died before he could give it to us. Helmut had gotten in touch and told us where to find it, which is why we came to Heidelberg to collect it."

The inspector's eyes narrowed. "Our team will have local experts verify the Vermeer's authenticity before we do anything else," he stated. "If it is genuine, then your client can file a claim with our government to have it returned to him—provided he has evidence to prove his ownership."

"But Helmut's letter—"

"I'm sure the courts will take the letter into consideration. But I am not authorized to hand over a multimillion-dollar painting based on a dead man's rather vague claim."

Vincent muttered under his breath. Zelda knew this was exactly the sort of situation he had been trying to avoid. If they had to wait for a court of law to determine its ownership, Roelf would most likely die before their decision was announced.

After they were done with the police, Zelda, Jacob, and Vincent walked slowly along a path running parallel to the river. Jacob took her hand and squeezed, bringing a sad smile to Zelda's eyes. This was not at all how she expected this day to end.

"I should call your parents and let them know that we will be later than expected," Jacob finally said, breaking the silence.

When Zelda stopped to talk with Jacob, Vincent continued walking along the path, his head bowed as if he was deep in thought. She watched her boss a moment, before turning her attention to her boyfriend.

"Are you sure you want to call them? They are my parents."

Jacob smiled. "Yes, but it was my surprise."

Zelda's eyebrows crinkled together. "I don't understand."

"I'll explain later, but right now, I think you and Vincent need to talk about what to do next. I'll wait for you over there. Okay?" Jacob pointed to a bench along the river's edge.

"Thanks, hon." She kissed him briefly on the lips before sprinting to catch up with her boss. "Do you really believe that Helmut wrote that suicide note?"

Vincent slowed down to allow her to catch up. "The police seem to. It does explain the burned paintings and why Helmut had the Vermeer with him."

"What about that old ledger that hulk of a man took from me? At gunpoint, I might add. That's a pretty good indication that it is important, somehow."

"That's true, but it doesn't mean that it has anything to do with a looted collection."

"Okay, but don't you think it is strange that he went straight for the book, instead of the painting? And who was he, anyway? And how did Brigitte know the Vermeer was there?"

"I wish I knew the answer," Vincent murmured.

Zelda tapped her chin. "Brigitte's presence must mean that Max is involved, as well. You mentioned that Brigitte and Max might be in a relationship and both admitted to working with Kurt Weber. And both are supposedly part of that network you refuse to believe exists."

"Was. Brigitte is dead, remember? Just like this investigation is."

Zelda shuddered. She would never be able to rid her mind of that image of Brigitte's flailing arms, trying to grab onto the loose stones before she fell backwards into the deep valley below.

"And what network are you referring to? The one a few sensationalist newspapers love to print rumors about? There is no network, just like there is no secret collection. Kurt and Helmut were cruel men who tried to play a horrid hoax on you. End of story."

"But, Vincent—"

"There's more going on than just this investigation. Theresa gave me an ultimatum last night. Either I move back to Amsterdam, or she is going to file for divorce."

"Ouch. What are you going to do?"

"Save my marriage, that's what. Losing Theresa isn't worth making a little more money. I was doing fine in Amsterdam, and that's where our life together is. Besides, Croatia isn't panning out as I had hoped. Maybe if I gave it longer, things would pick up, but it's not important anymore."

"And what about Kurt's missing collection? The fact that the Vermeer exists is reason enough to believe that he had more looted artwork in his possession. If we can find Max, I bet we will find the rest of Kurt's missing collection."

"Zelda, you have to learn the difference between pure fantasy and conjecture. Bad guys lie and for all sorts of reasons." When she started to protest, Vincent held up his hands. "Tell you what, if the Vermeer is real, we'll talk about it again. But even if it is, it doesn't necessarily mean that Kurt had hundreds of looted paintings stored away. And even if he did, we have no way of proving that Max stole the artwork from him. We don't know the titles of the paintings or the names of their creators."

Zelda held out her hand. "It's a deal. If the Vermeer is real, we keep searching. If it's not, I let it go."

Vincent blew out his cheeks and shook her outstretched hand. "Okay, fair enough. But right now, I need to sort out my Amsterdam office. Would you be interested in being my full-time assistant?"

"I'm sorry, but no. I've decided to apply for an assistant curator position at a new museum opening in Amsterdam."

Vincent's eyes widened momentarily before he began to nod. "A museum is probably a better fit for you. You're too gullible and naive to do this full time," he joked.

"At least I'll never be as cynical as you," she teased back.

"Hey guys," Jacob said as he walked towards them, his phone in hand. "I don't mean to break up the party, but it's almost five o'clock. Shouldn't we head back? I've talked to your parents and they understand, but they do want us to stop by their room when we get back to Munich. If they are still awake, they want to have a nightcap in the hotel's bar with us."

Zelda turned to Jacob and wrapped her arms around his neck. "Thank you. I'm sorry about today. You didn't get to climb the old stadium like you wanted to, and now I've ruined your surprise, as well."

Jacob kissed her lightly on the cheek, well aware that Vincent was standing right next to them. "It's alright. Besides, how often do I get to tag along on one of your adventures?" He grinned, bringing a smile to Zelda's face.

She leaned in close and whispered, "I do love you, Jacob."

He squeezed her tight. "And I, you."

"Okay lovebirds, shall we head back?" Vincent said, ruining the romantic mood.

"To be continued," Jacob whispered.

37

A Simple Gold Band

After Vincent pulled up to their hotel and dropped them off by the front entrance, Zelda and Jacob walked up to her parents' room, hoping they weren't too upset about their delayed return.

When her mother answered the door, she was gussied up in a lovely gown, and a wide smile split her face.

Zelda sighed in relief. "Oh, good. I thought you would be mad that we were so late. You look so pretty! Did you and Dad just get back from dinner?"

She reached out to hug her mom, but Debbie held onto the door, instead, keeping it partially closed. "The restaurant Jacob picked out was far more romantic than this, but I guess it will have to do."

Zelda's eyebrows knitted together. "What are you talking about?"

Her mom pushed open the door, revealing her father standing in a suit and tie, motioning towards a table full of food and champagne.

Zelda spun around to face Jacob. "What is going on here?"

Her boyfriend closed the door, then dropped to one knee. In his hand was a small box. When he opened it, the simple gold band caught the light.

"Zelda Richardson, would you marry me?"

She looked to her parents, both smiling and nodding at her, then back at the ring. She had never considered marriage, but she couldn't imagine her life without Jacob, either. Especially now that he was moving back to Amsterdam.

"Why ask me now?" she whispered, her eyes never leaving the box in his hand.

He grinned up at her. "I wanted to propose to you during our trip and figured our last night together would be the perfect moment to do so. I didn't expect you to go and find a Vermeer, instead."

Zelda twirled around to face her parents. "Is that why you flew over to Europe?"

"We were so excited when Jacob called to ask for your hand in marriage that he asked if we would want to watch him propose," her dad explained.

"How could we say no?" her mom added.

Zelda leaned back on one heel. "So you two have known about this for three months?"

Her parents nodded, their smile tentative as they gauged their daughter's reaction.

Zelda laughed. "How did you keep it a secret for so long? I would have cracked after a week."

"It was pretty darn hard not to blurt it out," her dad admitted.

When her mother jerked her head towards Jacob, still down on one knee with the ring held high, Zelda noticed that his hand was trembling.

"So what do you say?" he asked.

"Yes!" she squealed and wrapped her arms around his neck.

38

Flying Home Happy

During their ride to the airport, Zelda couldn't stop staring at the ring on the finger. The previous day had been a roller coaster of emotions, and she still hadn't been able to process them all. She hadn't recovered a Vermeer, as she hoped to, but Jacob's surprise proposal had turned a depressing night into a memorable one, nonetheless.

After a wonderful dinner with her parents, she and Jacob had spent most of the night cuddling and talking about their future together. Once he finished his project and returned to Amsterdam, they could figure out where and when they would actually get married.

She had shed a few tears when he left to catch his early morning train back to Cologne, but they dried as soon as she realized they would be living in the same apartment again in a few short weeks.

Now she and her parents were on their way back to Amsterdam for two more days together before they flew home. A wave of melancholy washed over her as she realized it would be months before they were together like this again.

She turned to take her mother's hand when a breaking news story on the taxi's radio pierced through the dark cloud forming in her mind.

"What is there?" Debbie asked when the cabbie turned the volume up.

"I'm not sure. Give me a second ..." Zelda's voice trailed off as she tried her best to follow the story. She could only understand a little German, but the repeated mention of Johannes Vermeer and Heidelberg caught her attention. Could the painting she and Vincent found in Helmut's home be the genuine article? She doubted the discovery of a fake would have made the news.

Part of her wanted to call Vincent, but she knew he was on his way back to Amsterdam to make things right with his wife. Now was not the time to bother him about the Vermeer's authenticity or searching for the rest of Kurt Weber's collection.

She also resisted her impulse to call Huub, knowing that it would be pointless and, in fact, could be construed as cruel. Even if the painting had been authenticated, it would take a miracle for Roelf Konig to live long enough to see his family's Vermeer again.

When she heard Vincent's name mentioned at the end of the news report, her smile grew tenfold. The extra boost of publicity almost certainly meant new clients. At least something good would come out of this mess.

39

A Profitable Day

Max Wolf gazed out at Lake Zurich from the window of his chateau, watching as a flock of swans took flight. As he recalled, they were Brigitte Vogel's favorite bird. He hadn't thought of her in months, not since he had declared to the Munich police that he knew nothing about her death or his bodyguard's alleged presence at the scene of a burglary.

Shortly after assisting the police with their inquiries, he hired a moving van, loaded up Kurt Weber's crated collection, and drove to a friend's home in Switzerland. Here he could simultaneously recharge his batteries and continue working under the radar. In the months since, Max had been pleased to see that neither the German police or national media had linked Brigitte's death to him or the Network in any way.

Although he did not have access to his own looted collection, having Weber's art close at hand made it possible to conduct his business. Luckily for him, Bruno Weber had an excellent eye, and the paintings he had saved were superb. Max knew several collectors who would willingly pay top dollar to possess such a piece.

He pulled out his client list, considering who he should approach next, when his phone rang. The name of a prominent politician, also on the list in his hand, lit up on the caller ID screen.

Max watched the wind kick up frothy waves in the lake as they exchanged brief pleasantries. "I am afraid the Vermeer is no longer available. However,

I do have several alternatives that I believe you will find satisfactory."

He began listing off some of the more well-known artists in Kurt's collection, pausing to let each name sink in. Based on his client's jubilant reaction, it was going to be a profitable day.

40

Justice Served

"Target is approaching the house!" Vincent murmured to Zelda, translating what a Swiss police inspector was saying via walkie-talkie. They were hunkered down behind a row of bushes on a hillside situated above a sprawling mansion, watching with binoculars as they waited for their quarry to return. As much as she wanted to be closer to the action, Zelda knew that if their suspect recognized her or her boss, the entire operation might be blown. All things considered, she was grateful that the local authorities allowed them to watch the arrest, even from a distance.

Sure enough, through the viewfinder she could see Max Wolf's sleek black Audi turn onto the long driveway. As soon as his car was through the gate, a team of police officers stormed inside and surrounded Max's vehicle. Through the walkie-talkie, Vincent followed the arrest and relayed the happenings to Zelda. As expected, Max refused to get out of his car, screaming that he had friends in high places who would not look kindly on how the Swiss were treating him. Despite his objections, he was pulled out of the driver's seat and pushed onto the hood, so the officer could handcuff him.

A smile split Zelda's face. She could hardly believe that this day had come, and fairly quickly, given how difficult it had been to follow Max's trail.

Shortly after the Vermeer's discovery made the news, Vincent had gotten in touch, his text message simply stating that it was "time to hunt." A long line of leads from trusted informants led them increasingly closer, until Vincent finally caught sight of Max leaving a rented home outside of Zurich.

He had followed Wolf's Audi and a convoy of moving vans until they reached this mansion in a village close to Bern. Through his camera's long-zoom lens, Vincent had caught sight of the movers shifting hundreds of crates into the large home. After he had explained that Interpol had issued an international arrest warrant for Max because he was suspected of trading in stolen artwork, the local authorities were happy to cooperate. Those photos of the movers were the evidence the Swiss police needed to bring Max Wolf in for questioning.

As she watched a handcuffed Max being led to a police car, Zelda felt a surge of elation, thrilled that he would finally be prosecuted for his crimes. At least, she hoped that would be the case. He was so well connected, she was slightly concerned one of his friends would try to arrange for his release.

She and Vincent headed down the hill towards the house. From the smile on his face, her boss was apparently as psyched about Max's arrest as she was.

When they were close to the group of officers surrounding their suspect, she noted that he was protesting loudly as an officer attempted to put him in the back of a police car.

Vincent began to shake his head. "Figures. Max is saying that he does not know why the authorities are pestering him."

Her blood boiled as she watched that sneaky man try to weasel his way out of a jail sentence. Would it work this time? She wasn't certain.

When the lead inspector entered the rented home, Max's cries turned to shrieks.

"What's he saying now?" Zelda asked her boss.

"That he is staying at a friend's place and the only possessions of his inside are his clothes and a suitcase. He swears he doesn't know anything about the crates stacked up in the living room."

Zelda chuckled. "I bet he doesn't."

Vincent laughed along. "With a little luck, the police will find his fingerprints on whatever is stored inside of them."

After the local authorities got Max into the back of a police car and drove off, they moved closer in the hopes of running into the lead detective.

When one of the investigators Vincent knew spotted them, he waved them over.

"You have to see this," the policeman said, a wide grin on his face as he ushed them inside the home Max was renting.

There were so many crates stacked up around the mansion that it felt as if she was walking through a massive storage depot. Policemen were busy removing the lids of the crates and photographing the contents.

Zelda couldn't help but gawk as she took note of the many high-quality paintings and sketches visible within.

"Could this be all of the artwork Bruno Weber saved?" Zelda asked, her voice a whisper. When her boss didn't respond, she turned to look for him.

Vincent had stopped by one crate and was staring inside as if his eyes were deceiving him. "I'm not sure if it's Kurt's art collection or not. But I have to assume it is all stolen, otherwise he wouldn't have said that he didn't know anything about the crates' contents."

"This doesn't mean that this network really exists," he rushed to add. "But I have been looking for this work by Claude Monet for several years. It was taken from a home in Amsterdam in 1941, and I know for a fact that it is listed in the Art Loss Register. I wouldn't be surprised if more of the paintings in these crates are, as well."

His tone was reverent as he gazed down at the piece. "The owner has already passed, but his grandson is still in the Netherlands. It will mean so much to him to get this back."

Vincent scanned the room. "Besides, I doubt this is all of the artwork Max has in his possession. He must have paintings stored in multiple locations." The disappointment in his voice was evident.

Zelda also took in the sight before them, yet refused to share in his dissatisfaction. "You're probably right. But with a little luck, we'll find clues to the rest in his paperwork. There has to be a hundred or more paintings here that we can return to their rightful owners. If this is Kurt's collection, tracking them down should be relatively easily, thanks to the detailed ledgers his father left behind."

"Zelda, Max is being turned over to Interpol. This entire case is out of our hands. We won't be reuniting anyone with their paintings—they have specialized teams for that."

"Oh." Zelda had trouble keeping the disappointment out of her voice. "Then I guess knowing these paintings will be returned will have to be enough. That's pretty special."

Vincent chuckled and squeezed her shoulder. "You're right. We should focus on what we have accomplished, not what is still out there. It's simply too depressing otherwise."

Zelda gazed over the crates before her, many holding masterpieces most museums would salivate over. They reminded her of all the other missing artworks she'd had the privilege of finding over the years.

Every painting was a puzzle piece that fit perfectly into someone's family history. The more puzzles they could fill, the better the world would be.

THE END

Thank you for reading my novel!
Reviews really do help readers decide whether they want to take a chance on a new author. If you enjoyed this story, please consider posting a review on BookBub, Goodreads, Facebook, or with your favorite retailer.
I appreciate it! Jennifer S. Alderson

Acknowledgments

This second edition of *The Vermeer Deception* (published in August 2022) has been revised to address several readers' concerns. In the original version, Zelda's parents and boyfriend were not supportive of her search for the Vermeer, something that I originally thought was necessary to add tension to the novel. Unfortunately, the characters' reactions ended up irritating many reviewers, instead of drawing them into the story. I hope this revised edition better fulfills readers' expectations!

I am incredibly grateful to my husband, Philip, and son, Jasper, for their support and encouragement while writing these stories. They were also great traveling companions on my location research trip through Bavaria. If it weren't for my son's love of funiculars, we probably would not have visited the beautiful city of Heidelberg.

Shortly after I finished writing the first book in the Zelda Richardson Mystery series, *The Lover's Portrait*, the discovery of almost 1,400 looted paintings and prints in a Munich apartment hit the news. A retired art dealer named Cornelius Gurlitt had inherited this collection from his father, Hildebrand, an art dealer who worked for Adolf Hitler during World War II. Several news articles about Gurlitt mentioned a rumored secret network of art dealers still actively trading in Nazi-looted artwork and that both Cornelius and Hildebrand were probably part of it. This fascinating story eventually inspired this fictitious one.

The *Dienststelle Mühlmann*, as described in this novel, really did exist. The information mentioned about Kajetan Mühlmann in the Vlug Report can be found on pages 5 and 12.

While Johannes Vermeer did make several tronies as marketing tools—including *Girl with a Pearl Earring*—Roelf's Vermeer is a figment of my imagination.

The rest of the characters and scenarios described in this novel are purely fiction.

About the Author

Sign up for Jennifer's newsletter to get a FREE copy of *Holiday Gone Wrong!* [http://eepurl.com/cWmc29]

Jennifer S. Alderson was born in San Francisco, raised in Seattle, and currently lives in Amsterdam. After traveling extensively around Asia, Oceania, and Central America, she moved to Darwin, Australia, before finally settling in the Netherlands. Her background in journalism, multimedia development, and art history enriches her novels. When not writing, she can be found in a museum, biking around Amsterdam, or enjoying a coffee along the canal while planning her next research trip.

Jennifer's love of travel, art, and culture inspires her award-winning Zelda Richardson Mystery series, her Travel Can Be Murder Cozy Mysteries, and her standalone stories.

Book One of the Zelda Richardson Mystery series—*The Lover's Portrait*—is a suspenseful whodunit about Nazi-looted artwork that transports readers to WWII and present-day Amsterdam. Art, religion, and anthropology collide in *Rituals of the Dead* (Book Two), a thrilling artifact mystery set in Papua and the Netherlands. Her pulse-pounding adventure set in the Netherlands, Croatia, Italy, and Turkey—*Marked for Revenge* (Book Three)—is a story about stolen art, the mafia, and a father's vengeance. Book Four—*The Vermeer Deception*—is a WWII art mystery set in Germany and the Netherlands.

The Travel Can Be Murder Cozy Mysteries follow the adventures of tour guide and amateur sleuth Lana Hansen. Book One—*Death on the Danube*—takes Lana to Budapest for a New Year's trip. In *Death by Baguette* (Book Two), Lana escorts five couples on an unforgettable Valentine-themed vacation to Paris. In Book Three—*Death by Windmill*—Lana's estranged mother joins her Mother's Day tour to the Netherlands. In Book Four—*Death by Bagpipes*—Lana accompanies a famous magician and his family to Edinburgh during the Fringe Festival. In Book Five—*Death by Fountain*—Lana has to sleuth out who really killed Randy Wright's ex-girlfriend, before his visit to Rome becomes permanent. In Book Six, *Death by Leprechaun,* Lana needs the luck of the Irish to clear her friend of a crime. In Book Seven—*Death by Flamenco*—Lana has to sleuth out a murderer if she is to dance her way out of a jail sentence. In Book Eight—*Death by Gondola*—Lana's sleuthing skills are put to the test when her boyfriend is arrested for murder. Book Nine—*Death by Puffin*—will be released in late 2022.

Jennifer is also the author of two thrilling adventure novels: *Down and Out in Kathmandu* and *Holiday Gone Wrong.* Her travelogue, *Notes of a Naive Traveler,* is a must-read for those interested in traveling to Nepal and Thailand.

The Lover's Portrait: An Art Mystery

Book One in the Zelda Richardson Mystery Series

"*The Lover's Portrait* is a well-written mystery with engaging characters and a lot of heart. The perfect novel for those who love art and mysteries!"—Reader's Favorite, 5-star medal

"Well worth reading for what the main character discovers—not just about the portrait mentioned in the title, but also the sobering dangers of Amsterdam during World War II."—IndieReader

A portrait holds the key to recovering a cache of looted artwork, secreted away during World War II, in this captivating historical art thriller set in the 1940s and present-day Amsterdam.

When a Dutch art dealer hides the stock from his gallery—rather than turn it over to his Nazi blackmailer—he pays with his life, leaving a treasure trove of modern masterpieces buried somewhere in Amsterdam, presumably lost forever. That is, until American art history student Zelda Richardson sticks her nose in.

After studying for a year in the Netherlands, Zelda scores an internship at the prestigious Amsterdam Historical Museum, where she works on an exhibition of paintings and sculptures once stolen by the Nazis, lying unclaimed in Dutch museum depots almost seventy years later. When two women claim the same painting, the portrait of a young girl entitled *Irises*, Zelda is tasked with investigating the painting's history and soon finds evidence that one of the two women must be lying about her past. Before she can figure out which one it is and why, Zelda learns about the Dutch art dealer's concealed collection. And that *Irises* is the key to finding it all.

Her discoveries make her a target of someone willing to steal—and even kill—to find the missing paintings. As the list of suspects grows, Zelda realizes she has to track down the lost collection and unmask a killer if she wants to survive.

Available as paperback, audiobook, eBook, and in Kindle Unlimited.

Excerpt from *The Lover's Portrait*
Chapter 1: Just Two More Crates

June 26, 1942

Just two more crates, then our work is finally done, Arjan reminded himself as he bent down to grasp the thick twine handles, his back muscles already yelping in protest. Drops of sweat were burning his eyes, blurring his vision. "You can do this," he said softly, heaving the heavy oak box upwards with an audible grunt.

Philip nodded once then did the same. Together they lugged their loads across the moonlit room, down the metal stairs, and into the cool subterranean space below. After hoisting the last two crates onto a stack close to the ladder, Arjan smiled in satisfaction, slapping Philip on the back as he regarded their work. One hundred and fifty-two crates holding his most treasured objects, and those of so many of his friends, were finally safe. Relief briefly overcame the panic and dread he'd been feeling for longer than he could remember. Preparing the space and artwork had taken more time than he'd hoped it would, but they'd done it. Now he could leave Amsterdam knowing he'd stayed true to his word. Arjan glanced over at Philip, glad he'd trusted him. He stretched out a hand towards the older man, "They fit perfectly."

Philip answered with a hasty handshake and a tight smile before nodding towards the ladder, "Shall we?"

He was right, Arjan thought, *there was still so much to do.* They climbed back up into the small shed and closed the heavy metal lid, careful to cushion its fall. They didn't want to give the neighbors an excuse to call the Gestapo. Not when they were so close to being finished.

Philip picked up a shovel and scooped sand onto the floor, letting Arjan rake it out evenly before adding more. When the sand was an inch thick, they shifted the first layer of heavy cement tiles into place, careful to fit them snug up against each other.

As they heaved and pushed, Arjan allowed himself to think about the future for the first time in weeks. Hiding the artwork was only the first step; he still had a long road to go before he could stop looking over his shoulder. First, back to his place to collect their suitcases. Then a short walk to Central Station where second-class train tickets to Venlo were waiting. Finally, a taxi ride to the Belgian border where his contact would provide him with falsified travel documents and a chauffeur-driven Mercedes-Benz. The five Rembrandt etchings in his suitcase would guarantee safe passage to Switzerland. From Geneva he should be able to make his way through the Demilitarized Zone to Lyon, then down to Marseilles. All he had to do was keep a few steps ahead of Oswald Drechsler.

Just thinking about the hawk-nosed Nazi made him work faster. So far he'd been able to clear out his house and storage spaces without Drechsler noticing. Their last load, the canvases stowed in his gallery, was the riskiest, but he'd had no choice. His friends trusted him—no, counted on him—to keep their treasures safe. He couldn't let them down now. Not after all he'd done wrong.

* * *

Death on the Danube: A New Year's Murder in Budapest

Book One of the Travel Can Be Murder Cozy Mystery Series

If you enjoy reading cozy mystery adventures, you will probably love the Travel Can Be Murder Cozy Mystery Series!

Who knew a New Year's trip to Budapest could be so deadly? The tour must go on—even with a killer in their midst...

Recent divorcee Lana Hansen needs a break. Her luck has run sour for going on a decade, ever since she got fired from her favorite job as an investigative reporter. When her fresh start in Seattle doesn't work out as planned, Lana ends up unemployed and penniless on Christmas Eve.

Dotty Thompson, her landlord and the owner of Wanderlust Tours, is also in a tight spot after one of her tour guides ends up in the hospital, leaving her a guide short on Christmas Day.

When Dotty offers her a job leading the tour group through Budapest, Hungary, Lana jumps at the chance. It's the perfect way to ring in the new year and pay her rent!

What starts off as the adventure of a lifetime quickly turns into a nightmare when Carl, her fellow tour guide, is found floating in the Danube River. Was it murder or accidental death? Suspects abound when Lana discovers almost everyone on the tour had a bone to pick with Carl.

But Dotty insists the tour must go on, so Lana finds herself trapped with nine murder suspects. When another guest turns up dead, Lana has to figure out who the killer is before she too ends up floating in the Danube...

Available as paperback, large print edition, eBook, and in Kindle Unlimited.

Death on the Danube
Chapter One: A Trip to Budapest

December 26—Seattle, Washington

"You want me to go where, Dotty? And do what?" Lana Hansen had trouble keeping the incredulity out of her voice. She was thrilled, as always, by her landlord's unwavering support and encouragement. But now Lana was beginning to wonder whether Dotty Thompson was becoming mentally unhinged.

"To escort a tour group in Budapest, Hungary. It'll be easy enough for a woman of your many talents."

Lana snorted with laughter. *Ha! What talents?* she thought. Her resume was indeed long: disgraced investigative journalist, injured magician's assistant, former kayaking guide, and now part-time yoga instructor—emphasis on "part-time."

"You'll get to celebrate New Year's while earning a paycheck and enjoying a free trip abroad, to boot. You've been moaning for months about wanting a fresh start. Well, this is as fresh as it gets!" Dotty exclaimed, causing her Christmas-bell earrings to jangle. She was wrapped up in a rainbow-colored bathrobe, a hairnet covering the curlers she set every morning. They were standing inside her living room, Lana still wearing her woolen navy jacket and rain boots. Behind Dotty's ample frame, Lana could see the many decorations and streamers she'd helped to hang up for the Christmas bash last night. Lana was certain that if Dotty's dogs hadn't woken her up, her landlord would have slept the day away.

"Working as one of your tour guides wasn't exactly what I had in mind, Dotty."

"I wouldn't ask you if I had any other choice." Dotty's tone switched from flippant to pleading. "Yesterday one of the guides and two guests crashed into each other while skibobbing outside of Prague, and all are hospitalized. Thank goodness none are in critical condition. But the rest of the group is leaving for Budapest in the morning, and Carl can't do it on his own. He's just not client-friendly enough to pull it off. And I need those five-star reviews, Lana."

Dotty was not only a property manager, she was also the owner of several successful small businesses. Lana knew Wanderlust Tours was Dotty's favorite and that she would do anything to ensure its continued success. Lana also knew that the tour company was suffering from the increased competition from online booking sites and was having trouble building its audience and generating traffic to its social media accounts. But asking Lana to fill in as a guide seemed desperate, even for Dotty, and even if it was the day after Christmas. Lana shook her head slowly. "I don't know. I'm not qualified to—"

Dotty grabbed one of Lana's hands and squeezed. "Qualified, shmalified. I didn't have any tour guide credentials when I started this company fifteen years ago, and that hasn't made a bit of difference. You enjoy leading those kayaking tours, right? This is the same thing, but for a while longer."

The older lady glanced down at the plastic cards in her other hand, shaking her head. "Besides, you know I love you like a daughter, but I can't accept these gift cards in lieu of rent. If you do this for me, you don't have to pay me back for the past two months' rent. I am offering you the chance of a lifetime. What have you got to lose?"

* * *

Printed in the USA
CPSIA information can be obtained
at www.ICGtesting.com
LVHW052144300724
786955LV00032B/781